UNEXPECTED HISTORIES

UNCOLLECTED ANTHOLOGY #28

JASON A. ADAMS   LEAH R. CUTTER
DAYLE A. DERMATIS   JAMIE FERGUSON
KARI KILGORE   DEBBIE MUMFORD   ANNIE REED
REBECCA M. SENESE   KRISTINE KATHRYN RUSCH
DEAN WESLEY SMITH

COPYRIGHT INFORMATION

Unexpected Histories: Uncollected Anthology #28
Copyright © (2022) by Uncollected Anthology

Cover Design copyright © (2022) by
RFAR Publishing
Cover art copyright ©
justdd/DepositPhotos.com

Unexpected Histories: Uncollected Anthology #28 is a work of fiction. Any resemblance to actual events, places, incidents, or persons, living or dead, is entirely coincidental.
All rights reserved.

"Human Business" © 2022 by Kristine Kathryn Rusch

"Ghost of Poker Games Past" © 2022 by Dean Wesley Smith

"Angry Earth" © 2022 by Leah R. Cutter

"Desert Scorpion" © 2022 by Jason A. Adams

"Embracing the Flames" © 2022 by Dayle A. Dermatis

"The Female Triumvirate" © 2022 by Rebecca M. Senese

"In the Banyan Copse" © 2022 by Debbie Mumford

"The Last Death of Angfil" © 2022 by Kari Kilgore

"Like Our Fathers Before Us" © 2022 by Annie Reed

"To Speak to the Gods" © 2022 by Jamie Ferguson

TABLE OF CONTENTS

HUMAN BUSINESS Kristine Kathryn Rusch	1
GHOST OF POKER GAMES PAST Dean Wesley Smith	77
ANGRY EARTH Leah R. Cutter	101
DESERT SCORPION Jason A. Adams	113
EMBRACING THE FLAMES Dayle A. Dermatis	131
THE FEMALE TRIUMVIRATE Rebecca M. Senese	159
IN THE BANYAN COPSE Debbie Mumford	181
THE LAST DEATH OF ANGFIL Kari Kilgore	215
LIKE OUR FATHERS BEFORE US Annie Reed	239
TO SPEAK TO THE GODS Jamie Ferguson	261
Uncollected Anthology	283
Uncollected Anthology Member Websites	285

HUMAN BUSINESS

A FAERIE JUSTICE STORY

KRISTINE KATHRYN RUSCH

ONE

"We do not do this," Madame Méric said, shaking her fist at the transmitter. The staff in the tiny smoke-filled office knew better than to speak. They knew that it was best to let Madame have her moment. Agreeing with her or disagreeing with her would not work.

Madame was, as the Americans would say, *a force of nature.* One did not argue with the wind. One did not argue with Madame Marie-Madeleine Méric either.

Rémy moved deeper into the corner near the door. He stood between two makeshift desks, covered in piles of paper. The other team members did not like all the paper—they believed it would compromise them and it might, if they did not have time to clear it out—but Rémy was thankful for the paper.

He had trouble in this room—in many rooms filled with humans, truth be told. But this room, with the transmitter, the knives, the guns—all the metal—it was dangerous for him. He had not told Madame who or what he was, but from the look she had given him the day he allowed himself to be recruited, she had known.

She had promised to use him only on special tasks, and she

had. She had sent him into the countryside around Marseille and along the coast, especially when she had been in hiding there, at the villa of a friend.

She used his talents gently and kept him away from anyone who would hurt him. He also had to stay away from operations that might lead to someone's death.

If he caused a death, he would lose his magic.

The Alliance did not traffic in death or assassination. The Alliance was one of the few spy networks that he knew of that was actually doing good work against the Boche.

The Alliance had allied itself with MI6, the British spy agency, and had sent coded information to them since before Rémy had joined. Madame had run the organization, which had had different names, since Marshal Pétain capitulated over two years ago now, and essentially gave France to the Germans without a fight.

The fae, if they had paid attention, would have been appalled. But they had believed—Rémy's tribe, at least—that the humans would do what they would do and it would have no impact on the fae at all, forgetting the tragedies of more than twenty years before, the destroyed homeland, the blood and gas and bodies all over their lands.

The fae were good at forgetting. Sometimes, he thought, they had more in common with the French capitulators than they did with the French resistance fighters. The fae did not like to fight. His own family had threatened to disown him when he had met with Madame Méric here in Marseille two years ago.

We do not get involved in human business, Rémy's mother had said, her tiny mouth even smaller with disapproval. *We shall be fine. We are always fine.*

It was the last time he had seen her. When he had returned home months later, he found the land covered with tanks and planes. It was some kind of staging ground for the Germans and the Italians. They had paved the land and put metal on it—the deadly iron.

Rémy could only hope that his family had gone elsewhere —*flitted* elsewhere, as they had in the first Great War—but he did not know. They had not known how to contact him, and he had not been able to contact them.

He shifted a little in the hot room. Madame was still waving her hand at the transmitter, as if the assignment was all the transmitter's fault.

He would have loved to blame the device, which he dared not touch. It held a place of honor near the window because the transmitter was wireless.

Its wooden box made it seem harmless, but once the lid was up it was a tangle of dials and wires. The Morse key was a button on the right, but he only knew that because the operators would tap and tap and tap, their knowledgeable fingers sending encoded messages all the way to England.

Sometimes Rémy thought those messages, the transmitter, the wireless nature of it all, magic. A magic he couldn't touch, any more than they could touch his.

What there was of it, anyway. His people had lost their powers progressively as the humans moved across the land, covering it with their machines and their pavement and forgetting the glories of the past. Even the fairy stories were fading, becoming codified into Germanic lies, and that had trapped some of his distant relatives in the Black Forest.

They had become lesser than they had been before.

The fae had all become lesser than they had been before. Even here, in the Gulf of Lion, where the land was still wild and the sea held sway. Even here, the fae had become lesser. Although their magic was much stronger than the magic in the Loire Valley, the Alsace, the—oh so many places.

He could not think of that now. He needed to listen.

Madame had finally calmed down. She would do what the British asked, what the *Allies* asked, even though she believed it dangerous and foolhardy.

Madame ran the Alliance with an iron fist, but she could not control her own allies.

Rémy understood that. He could not control his either. And he had made his share of impossible promises.

He had promised to get the refugees out of the coast before the Germans and the Italians arrived. He had thought maybe in the summer. Then the summer had slid into fall, and now, the gloom of November was ahead of them.

He had thought it an already broken promise, even though November was only a week away. But maybe, if he was creative, there might be a chance.

A slim chance, but a chance.

TWO

He had seen them from the moment he had first set foot in Marseille, nearly a decade before, those blond-haired uniformed men. Rémy had visited Marseille because he had fallen for a woman who needed to be near the sea.

He had thought her fae like him. She claimed to be something other. It was then he had learned that the water-based magical had their own designations, their own ways of looking at the world that had nothing to do with him or his people.

That had led to a fight—over what, exactly, he could no longer remember. He had taken her to one of the secluded beaches on the Côte d'Azur, before some wealthy humans thought of turning that entire coastline into a playground. He had shouted at her, and she had smiled at him—a feral smile, showing teeth. Then she had reached into the brown luggage she always carried with her, and removed what he thought to be an ostentatious black fur coat.

It had been hot that day—too hot for many clothes at all— but she had shrugged that coat over her shoulders. It fastened against her, transforming her. All that remained were her eyes, bright and dark.

She slid onto the beach, a seal now, her arms flippers, her legs becoming one, the feet splaying outward. She had barked at him. It didn't sound like an animal bark. It sounded like mocking laughter.

And then she had slipped into the water, splashing and barking until she was far from shore.

He had seen many strange things in his life, things he and his people often took for granted. But he had never seen anyone change form before. His people had lost the ability to do so generations ago. Otherwise they might have become sparks in the air or voices on the wind. Some might have become trees or rocks or deer or squirrels or something that was different from what they currently were.

But they had gotten stuck in this bipedal form, one that, some believed, was not even their natural form—without wings, anyway.

He hadn't been angry when she left. Her transformation had leeched the anger out of him, replacing it with something that took days to identify.

Envy.

He wanted magic as powerful as hers. He wanted confidence as strong as hers.

He wanted the freedom to live in the air, on the land, or in the sea. He wanted to be able to go wherever he pleased, without worrying about metal or human enclaves or towns or roads or being seen for what he was.

He wanted...he had always wanted...the ability, the power, to stop the humans from warring. From using all that metal and difficult violent disagreeable energy they had, and turning it into something that affected lives all over the world.

As a child, he had even asked—as children did—why his

people, whom he thought were all-powerful, could not stop the humans from warring on each other.

It had been during another of the wars, one that he later learned that the humans called the Franco-Prussian war, a war that had displaced his family from their ancestral homeland because, even then, they feared and hated the Germans.

He had asked his mother to step in and she had laughed and tousled his hair. *Mon trésor,* she had said in that small whispery voice of hers, *to use such magic, even if we had it, which we do not, would destroy the humans. The violence, the warring, it is part of their nature. As such, we would have to rip them apart to remove what they are. And that, mon lupin, would destroy us and our magic, too.*

Rémy thought of that often, even now—especially now, because this was the second great war of his lifetime, and the third that displaced those he knew. His people had long ago lost their ability to sail through these things, to hide their own enclaves, to enchant any human that came too close.

The magic now was a whisper of what it had been. Now, the remnants were sometimes frightening, sometimes useless, and only occasionally worthwhile.

It had taken him nearly a generation to figure out one of his powers, if—indeed—it could be called a power.

And he had figured it out in Marseille.

He had moved to Marseille for the first time to get away from his life, but maybe a small part of him wanted to be near the ocean. Back then, the villages on the Côte d'Azur were too small for someone like him. Humans would notice his extra shine, something that some of them called glamour and others called magic.

He also thought that maybe Marseille was close enough to wherever the woman—whose real name he had never learned —lived beneath the waves. He had spent a year in Paris, studying in human libraries, trying to figure out what the woman was, since his family did not know. His father thought maybe she was a sirène, but she was not, because her upper half was not human and she did not have a tail.

Rèmy had tried to explain that she had become an actual seal, a different creature altogether, but his family did not believe him, which was why he had gone to the libraries. There he had learned the proper word, which came from the Scots. *Selkie*.

He had tried to find her and he never had.

After moving to Marseille, he had spent days walking the Old Port, looking at the wooden boats, wondering if it would be worth his time to learn to sail one or maybe to accumulate some money and pay one of the fishermen to take him onto the ocean.

Maybe he would see a colony of seals. Maybe he might see her.

The question that he kept asking himself, though, was whether he would recognize her in that form.

And beneath it, another question: Would she laugh at him? He heard the barking of seals, and thought it derisive laughter, laughter that could, if he let it, destroy his very sense of self.

The first strong vision had appeared on a July day, warm and sunny, the light bright and crisp, reflecting off the waters of the Bay of Lion. Midday, so many of the boats were lined against their docks or floating out just far enough to suggest a tiny fishing fleet, even though they were unconnected.

He thought the boats lovely, something else he would never admit to his family. Some of the things in the human world he found to be not just useful but stunningly beautiful.

Humans made him see beyond the small world in which he was raised, just like *she* had. He had realized that his people, while special, were not entirely unique, and therefore he was not unique, much as he wanted to be.

That afternoon, he was inching on a conclusion, something that made him feel oddly more relaxed than he ever had. Before, he had worried about not coming into his magic, about not being equal to the others in his enclave.

But he had left his enclave and come here, and had learned, on his journey, that his enclave was not equal to other enclaves. He remembered thinking that he needn't worry because he had other options—long life, yes, because of his heritage, but he also didn't really mind the humans around him.

Maybe, he remembered thinking just before it happened, maybe he would be better off in human enclaves than in fae ones.

Then the storm came up, sudden and winter-brutal. Clouds didn't race across the sky and gather; they formed instantly and covered the beautiful blue. One moment, it was warm and sunny and lovely.

The next he was in near-darkness, with horizontal rain pelting him, and threatening to turn him into ice.

He pivoted away from the water, and picked his way into the street, feeling dislocated. He couldn't see the buildings. He smelled smoke and saw rubble, and heard—surprisingly—laughter.

Not the mocking laughter that the barking seals made, but true joyful laughter, male laughter, the kind that used to make Rémy uneasy because often it was directed at him.

He squinted, saw open flame despite the rain, held in the hands of a young man. The young man shielded the flame with a gloved hand while his friends laughed and pointed and made suggestions.

Rémy couldn't quite understand what they were saying. Their language was guttural and harsh, like English without the softening influence of Latin. It was that thought—that *recognition*—that made him understand he was hearing German.

The hair rose on the back of his neck and he resisted the urge to run. If he ran, he would call attention to himself. And he wasn't certain of his footing. The ground, which he had thought was level, was not. It was chopped up as if someone had taken heavy equipment to it. And there was ice in the rain, which he had never in all his life experienced in July, particularly not here, in the South of France, known for the beauty of the summer.

He squinted, looking through the grayness, feeling pummeled by the rain, but somehow not quite wet. He blamed that on his family's magic; he had learned young how to protect himself from the worst of the weather.

The men didn't notice him, perhaps because he was stock-still. That gave him a chance to study them. There was something wrong with them, besides the fact that somehow—without his understanding how—the entire Old Port had become filled with Germans.

German men wearing uniforms of a type Rémy had never seen before. It was black or dark green or something that seemed as menacing as the sudden storm. Their pants were tucked in their black boots, and somehow the hats they wore remained on their heads, despite the growing wind.

Their uniform was decorated with a red threatening *croix gammée*, a *fylfot*, something he had seen throughout his life, but never seen used as a symbol for a uniform, something to band a group together. They had weapons of a type he'd never seen before, but frightening enough all the same. Guns. Metal. Knives, all as astere and threatening as the uniforms.

Rémy turned back toward the harbor only to find it filled with half-sunken boats and iron-clad ships and autos along the docks that seemed slicker and dark and astere, just like the grimly laughing men.

He took a deep, frightened breath, wondering how he got to this hell, when someone touched his arm.

"*Monsieur, vous allez bien?*"

He blinked, the sun so bright it hurt his eyes. There was no wind, and the sailing ships out in the bay looked as lovely as ever. The water glistened, the air was clear and warm, and there was no rain at all.

"*Monsieur?*" the man beside him asked. The man was not blond nor was he wearing a strange uniform. He was not wearing a hat at all. A cap was underneath his arm, his shirt work-tattered, and he smelled faintly of fish.

It took Rémy a moment to understand the man. French. The man was speaking French, not German.

Rémy was about to ask if the fisherman had seen the strange men, and then, with a stuttering thought, realized that no one else had seen those men. The world had not changed in the space of fifteen minutes.

Rémy had come into his magic.

He let out a breath. He wasn't sure what kind of magic he had—past vision? Future vision? Vision that could be changed? Vision that couldn't?

"*Monsieur?*" the poor man was still peering at Rémy with obvious concern.

Rémy wondered what he had been doing.

"I'm sorry," he replied in French. "I..."

He had no explanation for what had just happened, at least nothing he could share with a stranger.

"You are wet," the fisherman said, "and covered in ice."

Rémy looked at his arms. Ice glistened on his shirt, but he wasn't soaked, not like he should have been in that storm.

The fisherman touched his own ears. "You are...?" Then he raised his eyebrows just a bit.

Rémy touched his own ears, felt the slight point that he

usually covered by keeping his hair a tad too long for any kind of fashion.

"My grand-mère," the fisherman said. "She too had moments like that. Such behavior, it is not strange here. But you look lost."

Rémy nodded. He *was* lost and confused and uncertain of what had happened.

"Germans," he said. "Did they ever overtake the Old Port?"

He swept his hand at the buildings, the roads, the docks, all looking normal and familiar, Fort St. Jean ancient and pristine, looking untouched.

He hadn't seen Fort St. Jean with the Germans, but then, his back had been to it.

"When?" the fisherman asked.

"Any time," Rémy said with a chop of his hand, as if his fingers could express the sweep of history.

"No," the fisherman said. "We have Germans, as you know. Marseille welcomes everyone, even Germans. But they have never overtaken Marseille, and they never will."

Rémy shivered as if the fisherman had sent him back to that windy, rainy, icy moment.

The fisherman raised his eyebrows again. "They will not, will they?" he asked.

Rémy shrugged, thanked the fisherman, and walked along the edge of the port, feeling deeply unsettled. The peace he had nearly found was gone, trapped inside his vision.

He left the port and did not return for days. When he came back, he saw the Germans, ghostly in their black (green? dark blue?) uniforms, with the strange angry use of the *fylfot* on the sleeves.

But he never went back to the storm, and he did not see the vehicles again—not for years. Not until he left Marseille and returned after the Great War, as the humans called it. Not until he was helping humans find food in the dark post-war times.

Then he felt the storm again, saw the same men, the vehicles and he knew them to be autos, not quite the ones designed in the downturn, but so much closer than the ones he had known as a younger man.

By then, he knew he had future vision, and he worked steadily to try to determine when those Germans would arrive. It took a few years, but he realized that the Germans he saw belonged to the Germany of the now, the Germany that was becoming more than an angry little power. It was becoming a strong power, strong enough to destroy everything it touched.

He had learned enough about his magic by then to know that no one listened to a future vision, because future visions did not come with road maps and dates affixed.

He could only guess.

As the darkness grew, and he learned the name of the *fylfot* —heard them call it a swastika, and heard them use it to talk about purity of heritage, heard too of his own people being removed from their German lands and taken to trains when their magic could not be pulled, he knew what he had seen. He just did not know the exact date.

But as winter drew closer, first in what the humans called 1939, then 1940, then 1941, he knew that the horrors would come.

In France, where the government had decided to ally with the Germans, Marseille remained a free port. Resistance movements arose there. Escape routes went through Marseille for the persecuted.

So many got away and then, by 1941, they didn't. They remained trapped in Marseille.

By then, Rémy had allied with Madame Méric and her people. She listened when Rémy said, not long after he met her, that Marseille would remain safe only for a short time. She set up branches in other cities, even lived in Vichy herself for a time, putting herself at risk.

She had taken the Alliance to Pau, and then, when someone betrayed them, brought them back to Marseille.

He flitted in and out of Marseille, helping his own people escape as best he could. He borrowed carts and wagons, delivered vegetables for one of the Alliance members, and, in the summer, took a horse-drawn cart filled with produce and two people into Spain.

His people couldn't take trains or cars. They had to stay away from metal. He knew that none of his people ever made it to the camps. They died on the trains, maybe only a mile or two into the ride, maybe even at the train station.

He couldn't even mount a rescue; if they had reached the train yards, they were beyond help.

He did what he could for his people, just like Madame Méric did for hers. Together, they found some solace. He believed she made more of a difference; she was working to end the human war.

He was saving what lives he could, but the opportunities were fading. No one could travel across the Pyrenees now. The Germans blanketed it, found anyone who was traveling without papers—and Rémy's people were always without papers.

The Germans were moving deeper into free France, and the French collaborators were working harder than ever to make sure that no one worked with the Allies.

Rémy had yet to see the Germans all over the Old Port, but he knew it was coming. Rain like that, with just a hint of ice, meant November or December, maybe January. He wasn't sure.

But the warmth had ended and the fall was over. Part of him fretted that this last group he was hiding would never leave France.

Rémy was running out of options. And until Madame Méric lost her temper at the English, he had no ideas what to do.

Now, he had an inkling of an idea, but it was only an inkling.

And it would require more magic than he had—more magic than all of them had.

It would require the creatures from the sea.

He had to find them.

And he didn't know exactly how.

THREE

Elise lived in a small stone house where two parts of the cliff face intersected, far enough away from the coast that the tide never brought the sea close to her, close enough that some evenings she could feel the spray on her face when she took her single glass of wine outdoors. She would stare at the horizon and sip, reveling in that moment of aloneness, knowing she wouldn't have it forever.

A thin road, barely wide enough for a single cart, branched off the cliff path. The path was treacherous, the road less so, particularly when she was on her bicycle and pulling the cart she used for her supplies.

The people of Le Lavandou saw her as an effective healer and midwife. They didn't ask how she got those skills because she had saved so many lives, more than any human doctor.

When someone asked how she succeeded so often, she said that healing was mostly about cleanliness and eating well, and the people who came to her not in extremis usually listened. They were her clients. She never called them patients, because that minimized them. They were people who paid for her expertise, and she liked to think some of them were friends.

Or so she had thought before the war. Now, everyone had a side and everyone had a reason for their side. Relatives in Italy —*surely the Fascists aren't that bad.* Relatives in Germany—*yes, we must apologize for them, but they are good people at heart.* Or worse, *politics doesn't have an effect on me. I fish, I live my life, I don't bother anyone else.*

We live in Le Lavandou, people said to her, *because we don't want to be involved in the world's crises.*

Sometimes she understood that. Many of the fisherfolk here had lost someone in the Great War. Although she knew they could no longer call that war "great," since this war was bigger—greater in the size meaning of the word. She reserved judgement about whether the war would be "greater" because the correct side won.

She liked to pretend she was interested in the way things played out, but if she was honest with herself, she was hiding as much as the humans she knew.

She hadn't quite gotten to her wine when the knock resounded through her small cottage. The door was a solid oak, part of the magic of her father's people, old enough that the oak's pain at being transformed into something other than its original form had faded long ago.

The nice thing about Le Lavandou—and truthfully, there were many nice things about Le Lavandou—was that her services weren't needed on an hourly or even a daily basis. Sometimes no one knocked on her door for a week.

But this night was La Fête des Sorcières, something her family celebrated when she was a girl. It was one of the few times her family could show their powers, and pretend it was part of the celebration. Witches were not seen as menacing during this week at the end of October; they were considered benign.

Or had been. Because La Fête des Sorcières was not celebrated in this part of France. She had always believed that did not bother her, but it was bothering her more and more, perhaps because of the press of the Germans and their violence, their willingness to kill, maim and destroy anything that was other.

Still, part of her hoped there would be magic in tonight's knock. She was feeling alone, separated from her family, and out of touch with the world that sparkled. She knew, though, that the world that sparkled was being systematically destroyed. She had no idea where her family was, and sometimes, she had a lot of trouble believing that magic even existed anymore.

She grabbed her bag, like she always did, and pulled open the door.

Rémy stood there. She hadn't seen him in months, maybe even a year. His face was thinner, if that was possible, and there were deep shadows under his eyes.

If she hadn't known he was one of the fae, she would have thought him a tired human, at the end of his emotional rope.

She stepped back so that he could come in. He did.

He wore dark clothing and thick boots. His black hair needed a trim. He pushed the door closed and watched her set down her bag.

"I know you didn't want to get involved," he said. "But I need someone with more magic than I have."

She walked into the small kitchen, knowing he would follow.

"Would you like me to make coffee?" she asked. People paid her in horded luxuries. Coffee beans were one.

Without waiting for his answer, she put a small ceramic pot on the burner. She always had one coffee press prepared for a late-night/early-morning visitor. All the water had to do now was boil.

He sat in a wicker chair near her ancient table. She had been right; he looked tired. He couldn't have walked from Marseille. It was over 100 kilometers away. So he must have hitched a ride with someone who had a cart.

She put some bread and cheese on a plate and set it before him. The water boiled quickly, and she removed it from the burner, pouring it into the press. She had no milk or sugar so she didn't offer it.

When the coffee had steeped enough, she pressed out the grounds and poured him a cup, which he cradled his hands around.

He didn't reach for the food or take a sip from the cup. Instead he watched her intently with his tired eyes.

"Do you remember the vision I told you about?" he asked.

She remembered that when she had moved to Le Lavandou, almost a decade ago, she had met him, and he had told her that his magic was small. Except that he occasionally saw the future. He didn't know when it was or what exactly would happen. He couldn't prevent it.

He could simply warn.

She had thought the vision useless, then. Her magic—a healer's magic, mostly—had a purpose, one she could access every day. But he couldn't control his, nor could he turn it to good use.

"I remember that you told me that should your vision come about, I might have to leave Le Lavandou quickly," she said. She remembered little else, because she felt what he had to say had no real meaning.

For all he knew, the visions he saw would take place hundreds of years from now. She didn't need to know about future disasters. She was dealing with enough difficult things in the present.

"And that's all you remember?" he asked.

She nodded.

He sighed. "The visions I had for here and for Marseille, they will come about soon."

She sat very still.

"The uniforms I saw in Marseille belonged to Nazis. Here, they belong to the Fascists. The Italians. They will take over the village, this winter. I'm sure of it."

She wasn't. But the uniforms were a new and convincing piece.

"Did you tell me that so that I would leave?" she asked. "I won't. I have two pregnant women that I'm monitoring, and—"

"No," he said. He waved a hand, as if he was dismissing her. "I know you will not leave."

A chill ran down her back. She didn't want to know how he knew that.

"I have hidden a group of refugees between here and Marseille," he said. "I've been having trouble getting them out of the country, to somewhere safe. And now, it is clear, I am nearly out of time."

She wasn't going to help him smuggle people anywhere. She had obligations here. She thought she had made that clear.

"I received an opportunity," he said. "One that you cannot tell a soul."

She smiled softly at him. "Who would I tell?"

He gave her a sad look. "I have trusted incorrectly in the past," he said. "I'm hoping I can trust you. If not, a dozen deaths, maybe more, will be at your hand."

She stiffened. "I am a healer, Rémy. I do not intentionally cause death, even if I were to speak incorrectly to someone, which I would not."

He nodded. "I thought as much," he said. "But these days, I have to ask. I have to be certain."

"People lie," she said.

"They do," he said. "But I've gotten better at reading the lies."

She wondered if that was true. But she didn't contradict him.

"Tell me about the opportunity," she said.

So he did.

FOUR

It took nearly an hour for her to understand the tangle of the story he told. He had refugees without much magic in a cave between here and Marseille. They'd been in that cave for weeks. The dilapidated farmhouse where he had initially stashed them had been compromised.

And then there were the people he worked with. The humans, who had formed what he called a spy network, something called the Alliance. They usually sent information to the British, but this time, the British wanted something from the Alliance.

The British wanted the Alliance to smuggle out a French general, Henri Giraud, and take him to the Americans on Gibraltar. The Americans did not trust General de Gaulle, who claimed he was running the French state from England.

De Gaulle, fully human, was using a human-type of magic, all smoke and mirrors and pep talks and propaganda. Because the Allies had roped him into their plans—because, at the time, he was the only leader outside of France who could talk to the French people—they didn't know what to do with him now, because he was getting in the way. He kept insisting on approving plans for France, even though he had no real authority.

The Americans wanted someone else. And Giraud had just escaped the Nazis, brazenly, getting out of a prison in Dresden all by himself. The Americans wanted to meet with him on Gibraltar, and maybe, just maybe, have him replace de Gaulle as the leader of France in exile.

Which was where the Alliance came in. They were to get him on a submarine that would take him to Gibraltar, away from France, putting him in the hands of the Americans.

Rémy told Elise repeatedly how much the leader of the spy network, a Madame Méric, did not want to do this, but she never turned down an assignment from the British. She had to keep the lines open.

She was afraid, though. Afraid of being caught, afraid of losing personnel, afraid of losing everything.

Others on her team suggested Le Lavandou as the place to launch a boat, so that Giraud could board the submarine. Le Lavandou was small and no one was paying attention to it.

"Yet," Rémy said. "But they will soon."

Elise shook her head. "I cannot help with boats or submarines. And I do not know how this will help our refugees. They will die on a submarine. You know this."

"There are selkies and sirènes in the waters here, no?" he asked. "They have the kind of magic that can encase an air-breather, get them through the water to a proper destination, like Spain."

"I am confused," Elise said. "You want them to follow the submarine? I thought it was going to Gibraltar."

"It will meet a sea plane in the middle of the ocean," Rémy said. "I want to bring my people out on the same night. If someone betrays the Alliance operation, then the Nazis will follow their people. If we do this right, even if there are Nazis here or collaborators or fascists, they will not notice *our* people. They can escape through the water. They can go to neutral Spain, without facing any problems in the mountains."

Elise stared at him. It was a bold plan, something she wouldn't have expected from Rémy.

"It would be dangerous for the mer creatures," she said. "If they got too close to the submarine or any of the weapons…"

"We'd have to tell them," Rémy said. "But I suspect they know."

She suspected it too.

"I am not a mer creature," she said. "I do not know how to help you."

"I cannot contact them. I have tried repeatedly." His cheeks were flushed, as if something about that sentence embarrassed him. "But you can."

"Why can I do it when you can't?" she asked.

"You have more magic than I do," he said.

She suspected it was more than that. "You have a history with them."

"With one of them," he said. "I don't know if they refuse to talk with me because of her. She thinks little of me. So do not mention me. But tell them that they're in danger too. If—when—the Italians come here and the Germans overrun Marseille, they will mine the harbors. They will bomb the seas. They will not care about aquatic life. Stress this. Tell them we must help each other to survive or we will all lose."

Elise sat with that information for a long moment. She had to assess how she felt, something she hadn't done in months, maybe years.

Did she believe that Rémy had the ability to see the future? She reached inside herself and came up with a strong *yes*.

Since that was the case, then she had to believe him that

they would lose their homes shortly. And they needed to fight to survive.

She needed to fight to survive.

She stood, feeling more than unsettled. Feeling a grief she hadn't allowed herself to feel so far. She walked away from the table and into her small living area, peering out the bubbled glass windows at the growing night.

She might have to leave here. She *would* have to leave here if the Italians arrived. They would not leave a woman alone, particularly one they saw as unprotected. And if they knew she was a healer and a midwife, then many of them were as close to the land and to the magic as she was.

They would know she had powers, however small.

They would try to destroy her.

If Rémy's plan worked, she could risk traveling with the mer creatures and going to Spain, even though she knew no one there. Even though she would leave her entire life to go there.

But, there were two pregnant women in the village that she had vowed to help.

Vows were part of her magic. If she left them and they died because she could not tend to them, she might lose her magic.

She walked back into the kitchen. Her heart was pounding, and she knew that even if he was wrong, even if the Italians never came here, her life would never be the same.

For Rémy had roped her into this scheme. And now, if the refugees died because she did not use her magic to help, she would lose her magic as well.

She suddenly wondered how much of her people's detachment had come, not from disinterest, but from fear of losing magic.

Ironic, then, that they had lost most of their magic anyway.

Rémy was looking at his steaming cup of coffee, his fingers tapping on the ceramic sides. As she got close, he looked up, his expression impassive, all except his eyes, which were sad and accepting.

He clearly thought she would turn him down.

"I'll help you," she said. "I cannot promise good results, but I will do the best I can."

He smiled, lighting his whole face, wrapping it in glamour and making him momentarily beautiful. He still had magic. It was just not a kind that could be used in this instance—in many instances, really.

She couldn't help but smile back, even though she was sad.

Because, even if they won, they would lose. Their homes, their communities. Their connections.

The world would never be the same.

She had known that, but she hadn't felt it.

Not until now.

FIVE

Elise sat on the headland, legs outstretched, hands gripping the wet jagged rocks behind her. The rain had stopped, but barely; the air was damp and so cold that her threadbare coat couldn't stop her from shivering.

She pretended that the wet didn't bother her. The wind buffeted her, bringing stinging ocean spray with it. She had learned, in the hours she sat here, to distinguish between the occasional spits of rain and the spray. The spray was colder and tasted faintly of salt.

She might have found this place beautiful, had it been summer, had it been warmer, had there been moonlight.

But there was none. For the past two nights, the clouds effectively blocked the moonlight. Sometimes she thought that a blessing; no one would see the fishing boats when they arrived to take Rémy's people away.

Sometimes, though, she thought it a curse, because inevitably, one of the fishermen would use a light, and it wouldn't look natural, and that might draw attention to the entire plan.

But now, she wasn't even sure there was a plan. She'd sat here, night after night, for nearly a week, and no one, nothing, not a soul had risen from the waters.

And there were no Nazis in Le Lavandou—not yet. And no Italians, despite what Rémy believed.

Still, she had to trust him. His human people, his Alliance, were here now, at a chateau not far from these headlands. Rémy was with them.

He would sneak to Elise's cottage at night, asking her if she had gotten in touch with the mer creatures.

She had not.

She was beginning to feel like a failure. Perhaps she was doing it wrong, sending out magical feelers, without really asking for help.

Mer creatures didn't always want to assist land dwellers. Elise had thought that a request for help might seem manipulative, but maybe she was making the wrong assumptions. Maybe she was treating them like humans when they needed to be coaxed, like fish.

Water splashed near her, and she jumped. The splash did not sound like waves hitting the rocks. It sounded like something getting tossed into the water.

Then a gigantic seal pulled itself out of the sea. It was bigger than Elise, bigger than most humans. It smelled of rotted fish mixed with ammonia, although not as strongly as the stench of seals near the colonies Elise had come across.

At least this seal—this gigantic seal—was alone.

Elise's heart pounded even harder. Seals were dangerous creatures, violent and unpredictable. One this big could hurt her, maybe even kill her.

But she had to think that this seal wasn't going to touch her. Seals didn't come to this headland. Usually the seals pulled themselves onto the beaches, sitting there on a sunny day, barking and cavorting like children, playing in the sun.

She didn't move, hoping that was the right decision.

The seal turned its head, its round brown eyes glistening in the faint moonlight. Then it leaned back, raised its long flippers and somehow brought them to its chest.

The flippers ended in hands, the hands pulled at the fur, and the fur separated from the torso.

The seal's fur fell away, draping on the rocks, the way a rich person would drop a mink coat, expecting some assistant to pick it up and put it away.

A woman sat on the rocks. She was not beautiful or young, but she was compelling. She had skin the color of the fur, brown and glistening like her eyes. Her naked body was heavy and middle-aged, with wrinkles pulling at her cheeks and a whiskered double chin that made her seem even more formidable.

Her breasts drooped, her stomach drooped, and her legs were thick and flabby. Yet her posture spoke of great power. Beneath some of the flab were obvious muscles.

Even though the woman was no longer a seal, she still had the power to kill Elise with a single blow.

"We don't take kindly to being summoned," the woman said in perfect Parisienne French, which surprised Elise. She would have thought that the woman would have spoken with the harsher tones of someone from Marseille or maybe with that mumbled influence of Italy, not too far from here.

"I did not mean this as a summons," Elise said. She knew better than to apologize to the magical—to any of the magical. It gave them too much control. "I come with a warning and a request."

"You need our help," the woman said, sneering ever so slightly.

"I do," Elise said. "*We* do, we land-based magical."

"We will not assist you," the woman said. "We will not leave our oceans for you."

"I would never ask you to leave your waters," Elise said. "We need help *in* the water."

The woman tilted her head, the way she had when she was a seal. Her glistening eyes looked exactly the same.

"You have caught my attention," she said regally.

Elise nodded, her hands gripped the rocks tightly. The wind had come up, bringing even more of a chill than before. The air smelled wet, not like the ocean, but like more rain.

"You know that the humans are at war," Elise said.

"It is not our concern," the woman said with the wave of a hand.

"It will be. We have magical with vision. They say that the enemies of this land will arrive soon, and bring with them many iron vessels. These enemies will salt the harbors with mines and will patrol with guns. They will shoot anything that resembles what they call torpedoes—"

"We are familiar with torpedoes," the woman said tightly. "You know we are. You know we've been mistaken for them."

Elise nodded. "That's why I'm telling you this."

The woman's head tilted to the other side, as if she was trying to get a new perspective on Elise. The rain arrived, chilly and filled with ice chunks.

Elise's exposed skin was beginning to ache with cold, but the naked woman before her seemed unaffected.

"When will these so-called 'enemies' arrive?" the woman asked.

"Soon," Elise said. "In the winter months. We believe that they'll come in November—these next few weeks—but we don't know exactly."

The woman's mouth thinned.

"Surely, you have visionaries too," Elise said. "They might have seen this...?"

"That is your warning?" the woman asked, making it clear she was not going to answer Elise's question.

"That, and the fact that these enemies, they will slaughter anything magical, trying to steal or destroy the magic."

The woman tilted her head back, revealing her neck as she looked at the sea behind her. It was not a human move; it was a seal move, made for a face that had a shorter forehead and was used to operating in the water.

Still Elise resisted the urge to lean to one side. She thought there might have been other heads bobbing in the waves—seal heads—but she couldn't be certain.

"So you want to flee these magical destroyers," the woman said, bringing her head forward again.

"I do not," Elise said, "but some of my people do. Usually we take them over the mountains, but those routes are closed now. We have an opportunity to get them to another country via the ocean, with your help."

"Why would we help you?" the woman asked. "If you thought we would do so in exchange for that cowardly warning, then you were mistaken."

Elise drew in a breath, feeling the cold damp air invade her lungs. She had approached the woman as if she were human or maybe a fae who was used to humans. Without doing any research at all, Elise had believed that the mer creatures would be happy with an exchange.

She had been wrong.

She couldn't appeal to their sense of magical unity. Clearly they had none.

So she was going to do what she had vowed she would not do—apologize to this creature.

"I'm sorry," Elise said, shifting, hoping her very cold legs would allow her stand. Wondering if she could stand in this growing wind. "I have wasted your time."

The woman waved a hand, as if the waste of time was of no consequence.

"You are not going to tell me what you want?" the woman asked.

Elise shook her head. "I have nothing with which to pay you, and I cannot in good conscience ask you to risk your lives for land-based magicals."

She slid back just a little so that she could brace herself better. The last thing she wanted to do was slip on the rocks into the choppy water.

"Do you think we cannot perform your plan?" the woman asked, sounding somewhat offended.

"I—" Elise felt a slight surprise. Her change of tone, which had been genuine, had worked in a way she had not expected. "I know you can perform the plan. I realized, as we spoke, that I cannot offer you anything in return."

The woman waved her hand again. That gesture had as much seal in it as human.

"Your warning is worth more than you know. We have had similar visions of metal items floating near our favorite fishing grounds. We did not know what those items were. We have a bifurcated future vision. Some of our people have seen others swim toward the items and explode into many pieces. Others have seen our people swim away. We did not know which would come true. We now know, thanks to you, that we can choose our path. Of course, we choose to survive."

That was a long speech that Elise hadn't expected. She also didn't know how the mer creature gained information about those visions—unless she already had it.

But Elise didn't know if the mer creatures had telepathic

abilities. It was speculated that they did, under water, anyway. Maybe they did above the seas as well.

"Tell me your plan," the woman said. "And I will tell you if we want to assist."

SIX

Rémy volunteered to open the villa from which the Alliance operation would start. The villa, where Madame Méric had stayed in the spring while the Germans searched for her in Marseille, had a view of the sea. But the villa itself wasn't easy to see. It was surrounded by pine trees and was very secluded, even for Le Lavandou.

Others had come with him, and Rémy let them do most of the cleaning and prep, while he scoured the area for food. If the organization ended up bringing General Giraud to Le Lavandou, Madame Méric wanted the querulous man to enjoy a good meal.

She had not found her run-ins with him to be easy or even civil. He believed most everyone beneath him. He refused to work with the British, so she had to lie to him about the organizers of his trip to Gibraltar. And, when she spoke to him a day or so ago, he claimed he wanted to lead any operation that happened on French soil.

She knew the British and the Americans would not like that, so she tried to warn them, but they believed they could control Giraud.

Madame Méric did not believe that to be the case, but she continued with the plan, even though Giraud's demands forced the Alliance to spend too much time transmitting messages to MI6.

Madame Méric was afraid that the Germans would track the transmitters, so she encouraged as many of her people to stay away from the office while the negotiations were ongoing.

Rémy took advantage of that to check on his refugees, and to gather food for the villa. Then he went to Elise, finding her at home, pacing, wondering if he would come before the plans were underway.

Her little cottage smelled of the sea. She had some fish soup cooking with vegetables that seemed fresh enough. She shared with him as she told him of her meeting with the mer creature, as she called the woman.

He knew she had seen a selkie. He wondered if it had been the one he had known, decades ago, who had disappeared into the waters of Le Lavandou.

Somehow Elise had gotten the selkie to agree to take his people to Spain. They would do so on the night of November fifth.

His stomach had flopped when she said that. He had told her that the Giraud operation needed to take place no later than November fourth.

He mentioned this and Elise gave him a withering look.

"I told her that," Elise said. "She told me the weather would not allow any transfer by sea until the late evening of the fifth. I assumed she knew what she was speaking about, so I let it go."

He stood and paced the small kitchen. He couldn't change things now. But the fifth would make matters worse, if the Germans or any collaborators got wind of what was going on. They would see another group of refugees and they might all be arrested.

"You're the one who told me to trust her," Elise said.

He nodded. He didn't even know if the Giraud operation would happen. Madame Méric had hoped it would not, because she thought Giraud a dangerous fool. Too many were risking their lives for him already.

Rémy let out a breath. His people would be on that headland on November fifth, no matter what. Giraud or no Giraud, submarine or no submarine.

There was no one to tell in Le Lavandou, so no one would report them.

He would prepare his people the way he prepared the villa.

And he had to trust Elise to make it all happen.

"I think they need to come here the night before," she said of the refugees. "That way, I can get them to the headlands easily."

He frowned at her. "If you're caught...."

She shrugged one shoulder, as if getting caught did not matter to her.

"We will not get caught," she said, and he could only hope that she was right.

SEVEN

Weeks before, Rémy had moved his people to a cave near the end of the forests of Le Lavandou. The trees would augment their magic, and the wildness of the area would make them as comfortable as possible.

The cave was narrow and uncomfortable, but fae, they could make anything warm and bright. He had to warn them not to let light escape from the cave's mouth on the dark October nights, and for once, the refugees had listened to him.

He had given them warm clothes and blankets, stolen from the Alliance's hoard, and he had given them what he hoped was enough food to last until they were to leave.

When he arrived at the cave on the morning of November 4, he thought perhaps they had fled or been captured.

The mouth of the cave was dark, the area feeling empty and abandoned.

He slid inside, terrified that they were gone. He didn't call out, though, because he wasn't sure what he would find.

The air inside the cave was warm and stuffy, and did not smell of the sea. He walked toward the back when movement caught his eye.

A young girl sat on a rock, watching him.

He smiled at her, knowing she was not young. She only seemed young. He recognized her.

One of the refugees.

"Where are the others?" he asked in the old language.

One by one they appeared, the two oldest, both men, with their long silver hair braided back from their ostentatiously pointed ears. They were thinner than they had been and actually looked older than they had.

The stress of hiding, perhaps.

Three women of indeterminate age, two with their hair cropped off because they had bartered for food in places other than Le Lavandou.

The young girl and two young men, all looking nervous and uncomfortable in the sweaters that Rémy had brought them.

He stared at the sweaters now, white cable over dark pants, and wished he had brought gray sweaters or coats. But it was too late now. The white would catch any light on the headlands, and he hoped that there would be none.

He would remind Elise to keep her flashlight low to the ground so that no one could see it from a distance.

He was shaking.

His day was shorter than he wanted it to be. The Giraud operation would take place tonight, and Rémy needed to be at the villa by dinnertime, even though he was to stay in the background.

So he was bringing the refugees to Elise sooner than they all expected. He had let her know this, before he had come here.

Now, he had to deal with the refugees. He did not know their names—their real names. Or the names they had assumed in their long journey from the Forest of Tronçais in central France. Too many of their kind had gone to Paris, and had died there.

They had been afraid of the French government in Vichy, not realizing how dangerous the Germans were in their occupation.

So this small group was all that remained of at least a hundred. Rémy could only hope that the others who had not died in Paris and those who had not sought out the help of his small organization had found a different way to survive.

This wasn't the last part of their journey. They would have to figure out how to survive in Spain, but that was not his problem. He had to get them out of France.

That was all he could do.

Gradually, the glamour fell off the interior of the cave. He saw makeshift beds made of clothes, a tiny fire pit, and a small box of food. They had been perilously close to running out.

"You will be staying with a friend tonight," he said, still speaking the old language, "and you will leave France tomorrow."

"By sea?" the young girl asked. She stood, and as she did, the years covered her like a blanket. She was probably closer to his age—young for fae, but not that young.

"Yes," he said.

"I hope you remembered that a wooden boat would be preferable," she said.

"I did," he said, and let out a breath. Then, rather than lie, he shrugged. "But a wooden boat is not possible. There are no nearby harbors and a fishing vessel can only go so far. We are taking you to Spain."

"By sea?" The old man asked.

Rémy nodded. "With the help of mer creatures."

The old man closed his eyes. He clearly understood. The younger refugees did not.

"The creatures, they have a boat?" one of the young men asked.

"They have an escape route," Rémy said. "You will have to trust them."

"It will require going into the water, no?" the old woman asked.

"Yes," Rémy said. He almost added, *If you cannot do this, let us know now*. But that was because he had become used to dealing with humans.

His own people were smart enough to know that they would be subjected to uncomfortable magic, and should anything go wrong, they might drown.

The youngest—another girl—looked at the others. "I don't like the water," she whispered to the first girl, the one who had aged.

"Ah, but you like living," the old man said. "To do that, you must enter the water. I do not like being away from my home, but I have endured. The humans are forcing all of us to do things we do not like. We shall survive."

The girl bowed her head. She was shaking harder than Rémy.

"We have an hour-long walk," he said. "If we see anyone on the path, greet them as you would a friend. Do not fade. They will get suspicious if you fade."

The group nodded. He had given them that instruction once before, and they had followed it.

He led them out of the cave, and onto the path that would take them along the sea. They wouldn't pass many cottages. The route was wild, but the sea beautiful—on days without clouds, which this one was not.

There was a wind and the air was heavy with moisture.

The selkies had probably been right: the weather would be difficult tonight.

Rémy didn't want to think about that. Tonight's mission was the human one.

Tomorrow's was for the refugees.

His heart pounded. He had spent years now on the knife's edge of anxiety, worried about being caught, worried about plans that might not succeed, worried about dying horribly as so many of his people had.

He had lost the ability to set those emotions aside.

So he concentrated on getting the refugees to Elise's cottage.

One foot in front of the other. One step toward the future.

One mission at a time.

EIGHT

Rémy made it back to the villa two hours before dinnertime, but his arrival was unimportant. The marvelous feast he had helped create by getting scarce vegetables and fresh fish had grown cold.

Giraud did not arrive as planned.

Of course he did not. The man was insufferable, impossible, and not worth their time.

Rémy spent his evening in the kitchen, but did not let himself pace. He tried not to think about the refugees, crammed into Elise's small cottage, waiting for their own escape.

Elise had greeted them with her fish soup and a warm smile, putting them at ease.

She did not put him at ease.

"I want you there," she had said.

"I will do what I can," he had replied. "But you cannot wait for me."

She had frowned at him and had not agreed. But later, he reminded her that the schedule belonged to the mer creatures, not him.

The priority was to get the refugees out of France. He didn't like that he had to remind her of that.

But then, she did not understand his work for the Alliance. He saw it as equal to his work with the refugees, maybe more important.

His country, the world, all of life, depended on defeating the Nazis and the Fascists. If they remained in power for too long, there would be no magic left.

The memory of that discussion, the silent observation from the refugees, the cramped feeling of Elise's cottage, made him even more restless.

He avoided the main room of the villa, where the principles on this job waited. Rémy tried not to speak to Leon Faye, an impulsive military officer that Madame Méric often sent in her place, her unofficial second in command. Faye had replaced her here, and he guarded the small transmitter they were using as if it were his personal property.

Rémy also stayed away from Pierre Dallas. Dallas had tried to recruit Rémy more than once to help with the airplane drops that Dallas usually coordinated.

Rémy could not explain his reluctance, so he tried to avoid the conversations altogether.

Of the leaders of this little cell, only Charles Bernis seemed to understand Rémy. Bernis was in his sixties, short and squat and opinionated. He had run secret operations for the French government in the previous war, and he often ran interference for Rémy.

Rémy had a strong sense that Bernis understood what Rémy was. It was Bernis who usually gave Rémy his orders, and occasionally encouraged Rémy to leave a small room when there were too many guns and transmitters and metal chairs.

There wasn't a lot of metal here, not even in the kitchen. The food, though, with the smell of the fish and the strong spices coating the fresh vegetables, made his stomach rumble.

He wanted to take some food for himself, but he knew better. He had learned to go without these last few years. He could sit until someone—probably Faye—told them that Giraud would not come and they would be free to eat.

If Giraud did not come, Rémy wouldn't just be free to eat. He would be able to go to the headlands with his refugees tomorrow evening.

The sound of car tires on gravel startled Rémy even though he had hoped to hear it. He stood, as did two others in the kitchen, and peered out the window.

The cars were not something easy to hide. Large, the kind that usually announced a person of importance. Allain, who had been put in charge of the meal, cursed, and Serge, who seemed to know how to do everything, muttered, "At least he hadn't put small flags on it."

"What flag would he use?" Bernis asked as he came into the kitchen. "The old flag of France? Or the abomination of Vichy: *Travail, Famille, Patrie?*"

Rémy suppressed a sigh. He did not want to hear that discussion again. Neither motto, the Vichy one that Bernis mentioned or the one from the Republic, *Liberté, Egalité, Fraternité*, reflected the kind of life Rémy's people had in France.

The team turned as one, only to find Bernis frowning at them.

"Prepare the dinner," he said. "We only have two hours until we meet the boat."

No one complained that the food had grown cold. No one mentioned that Giraud was late.

Instead, they went about reheating everything, all except Rémy who watched Giraud and several others mill around the cars. The rain had returned, along with enough wind to concern Rémy.

The boat would be heavy with that many people on it, and to make matters worse, Giraud's people were now unloading luggage. Apparently no one seemed to understand that this was a clandestine operation, which meant that it should have been scaled back as far as possible.

Rémy was not in touch with the fisherman who was supplying the boat. That was Dallas's job. Rémy had done what he could. As soon as the meal was served, he would slide out of the villa and go to Elise's.

There was much conversation in the outer room—a booming voice that grated, which had to belong to Giraud, and other voices answering. Bernis spoke loudly, as if he was trying to regain control of the room.

But Rémy knew how that would go. Humans were very concerned with rank, and Bernis was a mere colonel. If Giraud were anything like the person he had seemed in his negotiations with the Allies, he would not respect a single person on this team. In his mind, none of them would be as great as he was.

The voices continued as Rémy grabbed a crystal pitcher filled with water. They had all agreed there would be no wine on this night. There could be no temptation to drink too much.

The cover story was simple; they could not acquire wine of any vintage this far south.

Now all they had to do was hope that Giraud had not brought his own.

Rémy took the pitcher into the dining room. The room was small but elegant. He poured water in the glasses, and made sure the dinner settings hadn't been touched. Through the open double doors, he could see Giraud and his staff milling about.

Giraud was a thin arrow of a man, with a narrow chin and

flat eyes. Normally Rémy would do what he could to avoid a man like that.

As if he heard the thought, Giraud looked into the dining room. His gaze fell on Rémy and he smiled.

"I see, Charles," he said to Bernis, "that you have recruited some local glamour."

Rémy sucked in a breath. Not only did Giraud know what he was, he was calling attention to it.

Bernis followed Giraud's gaze, and laughed.

"We have no locals working with us," Bernis said. "You mistake a good-looking young man for someone with a bit of an edge."

"I do not make mistakes," Giraud said.

"Such folk," Bernis said, "could not help us if they wanted to. There is too much metal here. A submarine? It would kill them."

Rémy's heart beat faster. He poured the last of the water and went into the kitchen.

Only Serge and Allain remained, both putting the finishing touches on the meal.

"I would prefer to remain in here this evening," Rémy said.

"And I would prefer that every fucking Nazi in the world would fall over dead right now, but of course, that will not happen," Allain said. "I am cooking, such as it is. Serge is doing his best to revive the food. You will serve it."

Rémy closed his eyes. He knew better than to ask for anything from humans when they were under stress.

He nodded, unable to argue.

The conversation in the other room grew louder as the group headed to the table. Rémy grabbed a bowl of salad, made with a thick sauce to hide the wilting lettuce, and covered with carrots and beets and potatoes, and carried it into the dining room.

Giraud had taken the spot at the head of the table. When he saw Rémy, he smiled.

Rémy nodded, set the bowl down, and retreated to the kitchen.

"I do not like that man," he said quietly, to Serge.

"You do not have to," Serge said, as he poured a lemon sauce over the fish. Then he handed the platter to Rémy. "Serve it quickly. I do not think it will survive another reheating."

The fish looked delicious. Serge had sliced it and placed silverware on one side so that the guests could serve themselves. Around the fish, he had scattered boiled potatoes and more carrots.

Rémy was careful to hold the platter from the side opposite the silverware. He carried the platter out, and set it on the only part of the table with room, right next to Giraud.

After Rémy had placed the platter down, Giraud grabbed his wrist.

"Tell me," he said. "You are a sprite, no? I served with one. He helped me escape Königstein Castle. I would have gotten him out of Germany with me, but he vanished into the night, as you people are wont to do."

Everyone was staring at Rémy. He didn't know how to respond.

Then Faye's voice echoed from the main room. A loud curse, and a torrent of tapping on the transmitter.

Something had gone wrong.

Rémy used that moment to remove his wrist from Giraud's grasp. Rémy vanished into the kitchen, and leaned against the door.

"What's going wrong?" Allain asked.

He clearly wasn't referring to what had happened with Giraud. Allain was referring to the creative stream of curse words still emanating from the main room.

"I do not know," Rémy said, and sat down. His heart was racing. He had to decide what to do next. Flee because Giraud had figured out what he was?

But then, if something went wrong with the transfer, this team would blame Rémy, maybe even consider him a betrayer. He couldn't do that.

He had to pretend he did not know what Giraud had meant. If matters grew worse, Rémy would talk to Bernis and maybe get permission to leave.

A door banged. Serge opened the kitchen door just as Faye entered the dining area.

"The submarine will not arrive on time," he said. "We will have to postpone until tomorrow night."

Rémy began to shake. It wasn't just that he wanted to help his refugees leave. It wasn't just that Elise might not be up to the task of helping them.

But, he suspected, the selkies had deliberately moved the operation away from the submarine. They had probably been worried about their magic, about being hurt.

If this were a human operation, it would be so easy to let them know. He would use one of the transmitters, say that the operation needed to be postponed one more day. He would get a response and everything would be fine—or as fine as it could be.

But this...it had taken Elise days to contact the selkies and if they believed that Elise was toying with them, they might not help at all.

He threaded his shaking hands together and pressed them against his thighs. If only his magic worked on command. But he had not seen any future visions from these nights.

And wishing wouldn't change how his magic worked. It wouldn't change Elise's either. Hers was healing magic, which, if he was being honest with himself, they might need before this mission was over.

"Rémy?" Serge asked, clearly wanting to know if Rémy was all right.

Rémy forced himself to stand.

"Let us prepare the dessert," he said.

A bit of cheese, some old apples, nothing like desserts before the war. He made himself smile.

"After all," he said, "there is nothing else we can do."

NINE

The wind was ferocious. There was no real dawn. The day was not quite as dark as night, but so gray that Elise had to use lights inside the cottage so that she could make some semblance of breakfast.

Her guests were quiet, but they were helpful. They had just a bit of food, which they offered to share.

They said nothing about the rain pelting against the stone, so hard that she was afraid the roof would not hold.

All she could do was hope that the mer creature had been right—that the weather would ease by that night. She had no idea what she would do if the weather did not ease. She didn't know if she could contact the mer creatures again, nor did she know if Rémy's vision would come true in the next few days.

Elise was not cut out for this kind of work. Helping the villagers, she could do that. Coming in after a crisis, she could do that as well. A medical emergency, she knew how to handle that.

This? Defying what authority there was, holding people's lives in her hands, trying to time everything perfectly?

This was so antithetical to who she was that she wanted to

find Rémy, tell him he had to deal with this. She wanted to send the refugees to the headland now, but she couldn't do that, because the wind was too strong, the rain too intense, the weather too dangerous.

She had made a commitment. She had to uphold it.

So she served a meager breakfast and an equally meager lunch. Periodically, she would step outside under the eaves and stare at the sky, hoping the clouds would clear.

But in her opinion, they had gotten thicker, darker, more menacing.

She was trusting creatures of the sea to tell her about the sky. She was trusting Rémy, who for some reason could not be with her this day.

She was trusting these refugees to do as they were told, and they were fae. The fae prided themselves on doing what they believed to be right, not what they were told.

It was beginning to feel like this day would never end, like the night would never come.

And yet, Elise wasn't sure she wanted the night to come. She wasn't sure it would be any better.

She was afraid it would be much, much worse.

TEN

No one slept at the villa. First, there was a planning discussion—should they wait for the submarine to arrive and make the transfer in the middle of the night?

But the weather had grown so bad that no one wanted to even contact the fisherman. Even the non-fisherman among the group knew that no boat could launch in a wind that howled this badly.

About midnight, Bernis and Dallas headed to the beach, in the wind and the horrid rain, and spent hours, signaling with their flashlights, telling the submarine—if it had showed up at all—to return the following evening.

They returned at dawn, drenched and frozen, uncertain if the submarine had received their message, uncertain if their horrid nighttime experience had even been worthwhile.

At a lunch they had not planned to serve, Giraud once again grabbed Rémy by the wrist.

"You will come with me on the boat," Giraud said. "Your people bring me luck. I cannot effect an escape without you."

Bernis wasn't there. He was sleeping. Faye sat across from Giraud, and nodded at Rémy.

"This is the kind of day that tells us to honor superstitions," Faye said quietly to Rémy.

"It is not a superstition," Giraud said, sounding deeply offended. "It is the story of my life."

It probably was. But Rémy wanted no part of it. He just didn't know how to get out of it.

He slid his wrist out of Giraud's grasp and headed for the kitchen, making no promises.

Now Rémy knew, though, if he tried to leave this afternoon or even during the evening, his absence would be noticed.

He stared at the rain through the kitchen windows. He was so close to Elise and the refugees, but it seemed like they were in Paris and he was stuck here.

He wished he could tell them that he was sorry he couldn't join them. He wished he knew how to reach them.

But he could do none of those things, so he did the only thing he could do: he wished them the best of luck.

ELEVEN

By evening, the rain eased enough that the fisherman said the boat could launch. After all, he didn't have to go far; he just had to take the general, his staff, and his adult son to the submarine which would be, in theory, waiting a few hundred yards offshore.

So many theories. So much guesswork.

The rain was still horizontal and biting cold, with hints of ice. The wind wasn't as strong as it had been earlier, but it still made Rémy stumble more than he wanted.

He was walking with the astonishingly large group down the path leading to the beach. Giraud was in the middle of the group, only because Bernis insisted. Bernis, who was toward the back.

Dallas led the way, his flashlight playing along the rocky path. Faye had remained at the villa, along with Allain. Serge was beside Rémy. Giraud's staff each carried a piece of luggage.

Everyone had their head down, and a few were holding onto their ill-advised hats. The dirt part of the path had become mud; the rocky part of the path was so slippery that Rémy was afraid of losing his footing.

He was also afraid to look around. The headland that Elise would be leading the refugees down wasn't too far from here. Fortunately the evening was dark and gloomy, otherwise this group might be able to see that one.

That was the only aspect of this entire fiasco that Rémy thought fortunate. So much could go wrong. He was mentally berating himself for initially thinking that having the refugees leave around the same time was a good idea.

It wasn't, but he couldn't change this.

He couldn't change any of it.

They were almost to the beach before Rémy finally saw the fishing boat, outlined against the gloomy sky. The boat looked more like a hole in the air than a boat.

He let out a small breath, trying not to curse. The boat was ancient, which meant it was made of wood, which meant he could ride in it.

He hadn't wanted to. He had hoped that Bernis would help him make excuses, but of course, Bernis didn't know what Giraud's plan for Rémy was.

The group marched in the wet sand, moving slower than before. The clouds split, revealing a November moon that seemed brighter than it should.

Against the moon, along the horizon, a submarine rose out of the depths.

Rémy's heart twisted. He hoped Elise could see the submarine too. Maybe then, she could warn the selkies.

It was their only hope.

TWELVE

No mer creatures. Elise sat on the edge of the headland and peered down, over the rocks. The water was higher than it had been the night she saw the mer woman, the waves so choppy that Elise knew if she fell in, she would be battered against the rock cliffs.

And she was telling these refugees that they would have to slide into that water as easily as a seal.

The refugees stood behind her, wrapped in their sweaters, visibly shivering. The rain had eased, just like the mer creatures said it would, but the wind continued.

And then, in the distance, the clouds parted. The weather was improving.

Except along that horizon line, she also saw the outline of a submarine.

Her breath caught.

There shouldn't be a submarine anywhere near here. Rémy's team should have helped their general escape last night.

But...the weather had been awful. Maybe they hadn't been able to get him out.

She might not see the mer creatures at all. And then what would she do? Take the refugees back to her place?

And then what? Rémy had said that the Fascists and the Nazis would be here soon. If they found her with magical beings, they would realize she was one and she would die.

She made herself take a deep breath.

Nothing had gone wrong yet. There were only the hints of problems. She couldn't catastrophize. That was what she told her clients. Take it one moment at a time; a crisis was easier to solve in the present, not in the future.

The spray hit her face, weirdly warmer than the rain had been. But still, no mer creatures.

Maybe they had no sense of time. Maybe they were always late.

She really had no way to know.

THIRTEEN

It had only taken ten minutes to load the boat. Rémy had hung back, hoping Giraud would forget his admonition, but of course the man hadn't.

He had spoken to an aide, who took Rémy by the arm and marched him into the boat, over Bernis's objections.

Rémy let out a long breath. Curiously, he was not afraid. He had always thought that when he faced real death—real certain death—he would be terrified. But he wasn't.

He would die tonight. If Giraud tried to drag him onto the submarine, Rémy would die, maybe even when he touched it. Or he would die inside the submarine. Or maybe one of Giraud's men would use those guns they were trying to hide to shoot Rémy for disobeying orders.

Rémy had found one of the few seats, behind the prow. Dallas stood there, using flashlights to signal the submarine. The fisherman steered, and Giraud stood nearby, pretending to be useful.

The water was so choppy that some of the aides were getting sick, vomiting over the sides. The boat had barely gone anywhere. The trip was going to be a short one, no matter what happened.

The submarine looked huge and real now as the waves swept over its surface. It had risen even more.

Rémy hadn't expected it to be so large, but he should have. It housed forty men, all of whom were British—the submarine itself was British—but they were all pretending to be Americans, because Giraud, cranky as he was, refused to work with the British.

Apparently the British had gone along with this charade, because they wanted to please President Roosevelt; get Giraud to Gibraltar, and worry about the consequences later.

Rémy was probably going to be one of the consequences.

The wind toyed with his hair. His fingers grabbed the wet wood of the seat, which had soaked the back of his pants.

He wasn't cold though. The night had an odd beauty. Maybe it was the moon, which made the clouds a lighter gray. Or maybe it was just the air, so fresh and vibrant that it overpowered even the boat's severe fish stench.

It only took a few minutes for the boat to reach the submarine. There were men on top of the submarine, making some kind of speech in English.

Rémy didn't listen. He tried to make himself small.

But the aide came back for him.

"The general needs you," the aide said, taking Rémy's arm again.

Normally, Rémy would have shaken him off, but he didn't. He let himself be led to the side of the boat where Giraud stood.

All they had to do was climb onto the submarine. Aides would help Giraud and the submarine crew would steady him.

Some of the aides had already crossed.

Giraud, standing on one of the built-in seats, gestured for Rémy. Apparently, he wanted them to cross together.

"One at a time," Bernis said from the back. "It's too dangerous to go any other way."

Rémy let out a small breath, mentally thanking Bernis. Perhaps there was a chance that Rémy would be able to stay away from the submarine after all.

Still, Giraud wanted Rémy to stand beside him.

So Rémy climbed on the seat and looked down at the water, swirling near the prow of the boat. The boat's side was near the sub, but the front of the boat was in open water.

And there, Rémy saw seals—a dozen of them, maybe more. Their eyes glistened in the darkness, and it felt like they were all staring at him.

No one else on the boat saw them.

Giraud started to cross to the submarine, and an arm reached out of the sea and grabbed his foot, pulling him down.

Someone screamed, several men yelled, as Giraud splashed into the water. The boat rocked as everyone rushed to that side to pull him out.

Everyone except Rémy, who climbed off the seat and went to the prow.

"Let him go," Rémy said in the old language.

One of the seals, large and powerful, rose above the waves. "We never settled on payment for our favors. We need a sacrifice."

Rémy let out a breath. They knew he was in charge of the refugees. Elise had thought it odd that they did not want payment or any kind of guidance.

They had already known about this. The selkies had had a plan too.

Their magic was obviously different. No fae would—or could—ask for a sacrifice.

"He's not the sacrifice you want," Rémy said. "He's an old, bitter, delusional man who has no real power."

"The humans think otherwise."

"Not the ones I know," Rémy said. "They're taking him to other humans who will soon learn he has no value."

The shouts had faded, although they continued. People were leaning over the side of the boat, further unbalancing it. Some of the crew of the submarine had gone down a rope ladder on the side, trying to reach Giraud.

Only Bernis was paying attention to Rémy, and unless Rémy was mistaken, Bernis was understanding the entire conversation.

"Let him go," Rémy said.

"We need a sacrifice," said the selkie.

And there it was—the choice. Rémy couldn't think he was making this choice for Giraud. The man was horrible. Rémy was making it so that the refugees would get to Spain.

Death had stalked them all since this war started. It was only logical it would catch up to him.

"Then take me," he said.

The shouting stopped. A cheer went up, as Giraud clung to the rope ladder, the submarine crew helping him to the surface.

Rémy saw only that before he was pulled into the water.

The last thing he saw was Giraud, looking in his direction and smiling.

"See?" Giraud was saying to one of his aides. "I told you that I needed him. The magical have always brought me good luck."

FOURTEEN

Voices echoed across the waves, distressed shouts and then cheers. Elise looked toward the submarine, saw shapes on its surface, knew that the Alliance mission was nearly done.

A dozen seal heads bobbed along the surface, and a gigantic seal pulled itself out of the water.

Its flippers rose to its face, which slid off, revealing the human face of the older woman that Elise had first spoken to.

The woman looked at the refugees who, to their credit, did not make a sound.

"Have you briefed them?" the woman asked.

"Yes," Elise nodded. "What I could, anyway."

The woman waved a flipper at the submarine. "You see that ungainly thing?" she asked the refugees. "We will create an elegant ship in the water for you, filled with air. If you do not move as we travel, we will get you unharmed to your destination. If you move, you might pierce the bubble and drown. Is that clear?"

"Yes," one of the men whispered.

"Then those of you who feel courageous should step down

the rocks. We will pull you into the water, and take you with us." The woman bobbed her head at Elise. "You will not be coming with us."

"That is correct," Elise said.

"You are like your friend, putting human needs above your own." The woman shook her head. "It is a mistake."

Elise said nothing. She watched as one by one, the refugees climbed down the slippery rock face into waiting hands at the end of flippers. Hands pulled the refugees underwater, and for a moment, Elise could see them, illuminated against the darkness.

There was more than a bubble. It looked like a submarine made of light, complete with seats and blankets and a way to keep the refugees warm.

It might have been an illusion, but she didn't think so.

As the last refugee stepped inside, the light winked out. The wind blew hair across Elise's face, and when it was done, there were no seal heads, there was no other woman on the rocks, there were no refugees.

The real submarine was gone as well and the boat was heading back toward the beach.

Only the moon remained, scattering its November light across the ocean's dark surface.

Elise wrapped her arms around herself.

She didn't remember ever having been so cold.

She crawled along the rocks, afraid to stand in the wind. There was no one to rescue her, no one to keep her from falling into the sea all by herself.

She didn't stand until she reached the path that led back to her cottage.

Then she staggered up the path in the wind, feeling an odd sense of satisfaction—and the knowledge that she would never, ever do anything like that again.

FIFTEEN

Rémy woke on the beach, the clouds gone, but the air still smelling of rain. She sat beside him, the selkie he had known as a young man.

She looked the same, those big soft eyes, the unlined skin. Only she was naked. He had never really seen her naked.

When she realized he was awake, she barked a laugh.

"You are a fool," she said, "sacrificing yourself for humans."

Rémy nodded. He wasn't dead. If he was dead, he wouldn't be this cold.

"I told them, my colony, that you did not do it for them; you did it as payment for the trip of your people. That is correct, is it not?" She blinked those glistening eyes at him. He realized as she peered at him, her head turning unnaturally to one side, that she had whiskers on her chin—long whiskers, like those of a seal.

"Yes," he said.

"You are still a fool," she said. "They wanted to take you. We nearly lost half the colony to that iron boat. We saw it just in time."

"I'm sorry," he said. "I thought they would arrive last night. Timing changed."

"Humans are impossible to trust," she said, and stood, wiping the sand off her naked thighs. "We are done, you and I. I would say you owe me a favor, but you are too close to the humans. I want nothing to do with them."

"They're going to be everywhere soon," he said. "They're going to—"

"Have more ships, more of those underwater boats, more explosives. You have told us. We heard you. The colony is leaving this place. You will never see us again."

She started for the water.

"Wait!" he said. "How do I thank you?"

"We don't want your thanks. We're not doing this for you." She grabbed a pelt off a rock. The pelt was larger than it looked. "You—your woman—you were right about one thing. These humans, your enemies, they will destroy what magic they find. We cannot stop them. *You* cannot stop them. Only humans can stop them. So, I argued, that some of us need to work with the humans. That, I told my colony, is your sacrifice. Not the one they had chosen for you."

She slipped the pelt over her shoulders and, as before—all those years ago—it became a part of her. Before she completely transformed, she dove into the water and paddled out toward the moon, disappearing into the darkness.

Rémy sat up. He was cold and wet and shivering. But breathing.

Voices reached him. Shouts and surprise. The fisherman, Bernis, Dallas, they were running toward him.

One of them had a blanket. The others were saying something about getting him warm, somewhere safe, back to the villa.

But he couldn't stop looking at the sea.

She didn't rise out of it. There was no barking derisive laughter.

There was nothing except the moonlight on the water, and the wind blowing sea foam along the surface.

"How will we know if they arrive?" he asked as Bernis wrapped him in a blanket, as Dallas asked if Rémy could walk.

"They might tell us, they might not," Bernis said. "It is not for us to know. Our job was to get them out of France. We have done that."

Bernis did not realize that the question hadn't been for him. It had been for the woman, but she was gone.

Rémy had gotten her out of French waters, had gotten the refugees away from the shore. Maybe had gotten a befuddled general to the Americans.

Rémy would have thought it enough for the moment, but he knew it wasn't.

He looked up at Bernis, Bernis who knew what he was.

"The Italians are coming," Rémy said. "And the Germans will destroy Marseille."

"They've already found our Marseille office and the transmitter," Bernis said. "But our people are scattering. We need to do the same, Rémy."

He didn't realize that Rémy was talking about a greater future than the next moment. Or maybe he did. Maybe knowing the future was too much for all of them.

Rémy allowed himself to be marched up the path to the villa, where there would be a warm fire and soup from yesterday's fish. Maybe he would take some to Elise.

Or maybe he would go to the next job, although he did not know what that was.

Right now, what he needed—what he wanted—was sleep.

We do not do this, Madame Méric had said on that night weeks ago. Yet they had done it.

The colony of selkies, the Alliance, Elise, all of them. They had fulfilled a mission they did not want, in a war they did not want, in a world they did not want.

Maybe that was what hope truly was. The ability to believe in the middle of this kind of chaos, to see purpose in each action.

The woman—the selkie—she was wrong. This was not a sacrifice.

This was Rèmy's life. And he would do it until he was no longer needed.

He would do it as long as he lived.

ABOUT THE AUTHOR

New York Times bestselling author Kristine Kathryn Rusch writes in almost every genre. Generally, she uses her real name (Rusch) for most of her writing. Under that name, she publishes bestselling science fiction and fantasy, award-winning mysteries, acclaimed mainstream fiction, controversial nonfiction, and the occasional romance. Her novels have made bestseller lists around the world and her short fiction has appeared in eighteen best of the year collections. She has won more than twenty-five awards for her fiction, including the Hugo, *Le Prix Imaginales*, the *Asimov's* Readers Choice award, and the *Ellery Queen Mystery Magazine* Readers Choice Award.

Publications from *The Chicago Tribune* to *Booklist* have included her Kris Nelscott mystery novels in their top-ten-best mystery novels of the year. The Nelscott books have received nominations for almost every award in the mystery field, including the best novel Edgar Award, and the Shamus Award.

She writes goofy romance novels as award-winner Kristine Grayson.

She also edits. Beginning with work at the innovative publishing company, Pulphouse, followed by her award-winning tenure at *The Magazine of Fantasy & Science Fiction*, she took fifteen years off before returning to editing with the original anthology series *Fiction River,* published by WMG Publishing. She acts as series editor with her husband, writer Dean Wesley Smith.

To keep up with everything she does, go to kriswrites.com and sign up for her newsletter. To track her many pen names and series, see their individual websites (krisnelscott.com, kristinegrayson.com, retrievalartist.com, divingintothewreck.com, fictionriver.com, pulphousemagazine.com).

GHOST OF POKER GAMES PAST

A POKER BOY STORY

DEAN WESLEY SMITH

CHAPTER ONE

Someday I will learn that when I think I am having an uneventful night, it never turns out that way. Just flat never.

My night started at the Golden Nugget poker room in downtown Las Vegas. I hadn't visited that room for maybe six months, but it was a good room and I sort of felt, as Poker Boy, a superhero of poker, I should visit all the poker rooms in Vegas at least a couple times a year. And all the ones in California, Oregon, and Nevada at least once a year. Some nights I jumped from two or three of the small rooms, spending an hour in each.

The Golden Nugget room held eighteen tables and three times a day had some sort of tournament going on three of those tables. It had a low ceiling, like most older hotel poker rooms, and was decorated in dark mahogany, with a dark carpet and lighter textured wallpaper between the mahogany columns.

I liked the place. It just felt good.

When the room was crowded, as it was on this Thursday, it took some squeezing around chairs and other players to get to a table along the inside wall. Part of the charm is how I figured it. I spent a lot of time elbow to elbow with other poker players. Being crowded was just part of the game.

I had found a very nice 5-10 no-limit game, and was enjoying taking the tourists' money while pretending everything I was doing was luck. People said I was fun to play with, and I tried to play up that image. It certainly helped my bank accounts.

I planned on being here until my girlfriend Patty got off work at ten from the MGM Grand front desk. We had a late dinner planned at a new place in the Resorts World Las Vegas that we had been hearing about and I was looking forward to the meal and the time with Patty.

I was about to fold a two-three not-suited when suddenly I found myself in a very different room.

Maybe four tables, lots and lots of smoke in the air and the five at the table with me were all smoking, one a very nasty-smelling cigar. There hadn't been smoking in poker rooms since the turn of the century.

I glanced down at the chips I had in front of me that were larger than normal chips just slightly, and I had them racked in a wooden rack and sitting in front of me.

Everyone had their chips in a wooden rack as well. Just how it was done in a certain time in history, but not in modern poker. Racks were all plastic and only used to carry chips to and from a table. Racks were not allowed on a table.

And everyone around me and in the rest of the four-table room was dressed in old-fashioned suits, with ties and all.

I had started off the night in my black leather coat, a silk shirt under it, and jeans. Now I wore a black suit, a Fedora black hat, and a black tie. All matched perfectly over a white shirt that felt suddenly like it had a little too much starch in certain places.

I took a deep breath to calm my heart. I didn't have a sense of immediate danger, and the tables of poker just all looked normal.

My table was playing Seven Card Stud, a game I was pretty good at, but hadn't played in years, since it was pretty much out of fashion in 2022.

Then I noticed the heat.

Stifling heat.

I could see a lot of very old-fashioned slot machines in rows between the poker room and the wide-open doors leading out to the street.

Numbers of men, almost all men in fact, sat at those machines, pulling the arm on the machine to make the wheels spin.

The only women in the place were two well-built women with low-cut blouses and short skirts with nylons and high heels carrying a large wooden tray of cigars and cigarettes.

And everyone around me was sweating as a number of large fans in the corners blew the smoke around, but did little to drop the temperature.

Outside it was clearly early evening, and a lot of very large cars were going by, and couples strolling on the sidewalks.

The bet of 25 cents was to me and I folded my cards, even though it was clear I had a pretty good hand.

I picked up the wooden rack of chips and headed for what looked to be a cashier's cage just outside the room.

I cashed in for one-hundred-and-twenty-seven dollars, shoved the money in my otherwise empty pockets, and went out on the sidewalk.

I recognized instantly where I was at.

Fremont Street in downtown Las Vegas.

I had been playing in the old poker room in the Golden Gate. Those poker tables in there hadn't lasted more than a few years.

The train station was still at the end the street on my left and a few other old casinos I had seen in pictures were stretched along the street to my right.

"Before 1951," I said softly to myself, since the Plaza Hotel and Casino had replaced the train station at that point. But I knew this wasn't much before that point. This did not look like war pictures of this city.

What in the world had happened?

Who had brought me here and why?

I had been yanked back in the past once before and had not enjoyed it. This time around I was managing to keep the panic under control for the moment, but there was no doubt I needed help. I knew nothing about time travel, even though I had met Father Time. All I knew was that the gods and superheroes all feared time travel for the problems it could cause.

I moved around the corner onto Main Street, which was not as full of people as Fremont, and got to a place I could take myself out of time. That was a fun skill I had developed that allowed me to step between an instant in time, making everyone around me seem to freeze.

All the sounds of the night, the car horns, the engines, the slot machines' bells coming from open casino doors, vanished.

"Stan of 2022," I said, looking up at the sky slightly. "Need a little help?"

The last time I had been here, I had called for Stan and ended up trying to explain to Stan, the God of Poker, that I worked for him in the future. Had not been fun.

"What the hell?" Stan said as he appeared inside my bubble and looked around.

This was my Stan, dressed in tan slacks, a tan sweater over a white shirt, and loafers. In 2022 he could blend into any crowd and just vanish. Here, in this time, he would stand out like a flashing sign.

"You tell me?" I said, sort of indicating the older cars and the old train station where the Plaza Hotel was supposed to be. "I was playing in a great game in the Nugget when I suddenly found myself dressed like this, in a game in the old Golden Gate, or whatever it is called at this point in time."

"It's October 1950," Stan said. "And you look good. Sort of evil, but good."

"Thanks," I said. "I think."

Stan looked around, clearly puzzled. "There are very few gods who can travel in time. So I'm going to go talk with Laverne and figure out why this is going on. I will be back. Don't mess up any timelines while I am gone."

And he vanished.

And for the moment I decided to just stand there, out of time, with everything around me frozen, trying to get my heartbeat down to just racing speed.

CHAPTER TWO

Stan showed up with Laverne in under a minute, but since this was time travel, for all I knew a few months had passed back in the present while they figured this out. More than likely not, but as little as I knew about time travel, anything was possible.

Laverne had on her standard business suit with her long brown hair pulled back tight off her head, making her look even more stern than normal. She glanced around for an instant, then said, "Well, damn."

Now I have worked with Laverne, Lady Luck herself, numbers of times, and every time, without fail, that I heard her swear, things were not good.

"Just ahead of the gate, huh?" Stan said.

Laverne nodded and I just stood there, clueless. Typical for me in the presence of two gods.

"Someone is trying to alter the fixed-point," Laverne said.

"What do they have against Las Vegas?" Stan asked, shaking his head.

"Explanation, please?" I said.

"In about two hours," Stan said, "at that table you were at, a fight breaks out between a cheater and two others at the table. Two are killed and the fight sparks a fire that destroys this entire block of the city, killing hundreds more."

"I don't remember anything about that," I said.

"Because it happened in another timeline," Laverne said. "In that timeline the fight and the fire gave Las Vegas the reputation of being dangerous, since entire families were killed in the fire. And the fact that it is becoming a mob town didn't help. So tourists stayed away and eventually the town became nothing more than a stop on the highway between Utah and California."

"Train station stayed right there," Stan said, "and the mob casinos out on the strip were shut down and finally torn down. Half of the buildings on this street are abandoned or torn down or burnt down and they call Las Vegas mostly a ghost town in 2022 in that timeline."

"Holy shit," I said, trying to imagine the vibrant, alive city that I knew and loved ending up like that.

"So how did you stop it the first time?"

"I sat in the game," Stan said. "Spotted the cheater and got him out of the game before anyone else figured out what he was doing and the fight could get started. I still have a very clear memory of that."

"So is something going to happen to you?" I asked.

Stan shook his head. "I just joined that game now, taking the seat you must have left. My memory remains the same. I'll have the cheater out of the casino and into the street in about thirty minutes."

This was not making any sense at all. "If that is the case, why am I here? And who brought me back through time?"

"This is a fixed point in time," Laverne said. "The event at that table changes everything about this town. And a lot of other events into the future as well. Please stay inside this time bubble

Ghost of Poker Games Past 87

and let me talk to Chronos and a few others who might know what is happening and why."

"Take your time," I said.

She wasn't smiling when she vanished.

"Good luck," Stan said. "I can't help you, I'm afraid."

And with that he vanished as well.

So I just stood there on Main Street of Las Vegas in October 1950, in a time bubble so nothing was moving around me.

Sometimes, as a superhero, things just got weird. But I had to admit, there was no getting used to this level of complete weirdness.

CHAPTER THREE

Since no time was moving around me, it felt much longer than the actual three minutes it took for Laverne to return. She didn't look happy. Lady Luck not looking happy always sent chills up my spine. After all, I was a poker player.

"It seems," she said, "that from the time historians that I have talked to, Stan didn't clear up the major fixed-point in time by just getting the cheater out of the equation. He just delayed it."

"Stopping the fight wasn't enough?" I asked.

She shook her head. "This time around we have to stop and remove the fighters," Laverne said. "Time itself is like a river and it always finds a way. Now the only way to really cure this fixed-point in time, change the course of time and set it into the path to the future, is to let the fight start."

"And stop it before people die?" I asked. "And the place burns down?"

"Exactly," Laverne said.

"Can't Stan in there just let it keep going?"

"No," Laverne said. "The Time Board brought you back here to continue what Stan started."

"There is a Time Board?" I asked. I thought over the last decade I had learned a lot about superheroes and the gods. Seems I had missed something. More than likely a lot of somethings.

"The Time Board very seldom acts," she said. "But they need you now to take this point in time and change the flow. Missing will not only destroy Las Vegas, but it seems there are a few world wars that will happen as well."

No pressure was what I wanted to say.

Instead, I managed to take a deep breath and then said, "Well, people do love their gambling."

Laverne, ever serious, since she is Lady Luck, just shook her head and went on.

"As soon as the Stan of this time gets the cheater out into the street, you need to go in and take one of their seats at that table."

"Then what do I do?"

"Cheat," Lady Luck said. "And after a time, let them catch you."

"Cheat?" Not sure, but I think my voice squeaked like I was a teenager asking a girl out on a date.

She nodded. "We want you to cheat and make sure they catch you. And the moment one of the men at the table goes for his gun inside his coat, freeze time before he shoots you."

"Now that's a plan," I said, managing to keep my voice normal and level for the full effect of the sarcasm.

"A representative of the Time Board and I will jump in, take over the bubble, and make sure the timeline flows the way it needs to flow."

I nodded. "I'm going to be using time bubbles to help myself cheat, so don't jump the gun, so to speak."

"Call me when the moment comes," she said.

I thought for a moment Lady Luck might wish me good luck, but instead she just vanished.

I let myself take a few deep breaths before dropping the time bubble around me and letting in the noise of a busy night in 1950 Las Vegas.

CHAPTER FOUR

I went across Main Street and to the platform of the train station where I could see the front door of the Golden Gate Casino. Farther up Fremont Street were two other smaller gaming places and then the Golden Nugget. Beyond that the Four Queens. All of them had their doors open.

On the other side of Fremont was two smaller casinos and then the Apache Club. Beyond that the Fremont Casino.

The street was full of large sedans, the kind with slick vinyl seats that with every corner you could slide around inside like a pinball bouncing off bumpers.

If I knew cars, old classic cars, I bet I would be really enjoying this moment, but I didn't know a make or model or year of any of them. All I knew was that this point in time was a very few short years after the end of World War II.

And somehow those monster cars managed to not bump into each other or any of the pedestrians just crossing the street at will, mostly half-drunk.

All the men were dressed like I was, suit, vest, slacks, matching plain tie, and white shirt. My black shoes were dusty, even though both Main Street and Fremont Street were paved.

The only women to be seen were hanging onto men's arms.

And the street was well-lit but not like it would be over the next seventy years.

I really wanted to ditch the jacket and vest in the heat, but no one else was, so I just stood there and sweated until Stan finally brought a guy out of the Golden Gate and turned up the street away from me.

Within a minute I was back in the Golden Gate and asking for a chair in at the table Stan and the cheater had just left.

I handed one of the two in charge of the room the money in my pocket and he brought me a wooden rack of chips that I set in front of me.

Seems as if the two fighters were to my left. They both wore suits similar to mine. Dark cloth, dark hats, dark ties. The one closest to me had a scar across his cheek and both looked a lot like mob, or what I imagined a mob guy would look like in 1950.

The room was still filled with smoke and the two women with low-cut blouses and carrying big trays were doing their best to keep the cigarettes and cigars flowing and lit.

Seven Card Stud is played by first dealing each player two cards down and one card up. Then we bet.

After that three more up cards, each one a betting round, then the last card was down.

Both my first two hands looked horrible, but I bet one and called the second all the way to the last card, letting the other four at the table know I was here to play and not real bright.

I lost both hands.

Next hand I did the same, only this time I cheated, stopping time and making my hand better. I did that for the next four hands, seeming to win all four just out of the blue.

And the two beside me were getting angry, I could sense it. The one guy closest to me just kept stroking the scar on his cheek which I took to mean as a threat. And to be honest, it was threatening.

So the next hand I waited to stop time until one of them had looked at their two down cards, then I took the best one and put it in my hand.

I heard mumbling after that hand of cheating, so the next hand I let the guy with the scar see me pull a card from my sleeve.

He shoved back from the table, knocking his chair into the fan against the wall, and shouted "Cheater!"

With that, his hand went into his coat and the guy beside him stood and did the same.

My heart was beating about as fast as I had ever felt it beat.

I froze time, then shouted "Laverne!"

The guy with the scar had his gun out of his jacket, the other guy wasn't far behind. Both guns looked nasty. I hated anything to do with guns.

Laverne appeared beside me, along with a guy dressed in green slacks, a white golf shirt, and a golf glove on his left hand.

"Is the timing right?" Laverne asked the golf guy.

"Perfect," the golf guy said. He pointed to the chair knocking the old electrical fan over. "Fire sparks from there. These two mob boys kill both Poker Boy here and the dealer and wound about five others, including one of the cigar girls. Six others in here have guns and the entire thing breaks out into the street where a young child is wounded and his father killed."

"Can we take care of it?" Laverne asked.

The golf guy moved over to the fan and unplugged it, sat it upright and then looked around. "We can."

Somehow, I managed to just stand there and watch and not even say anything stupid.

Laverne turned to me and said, "Thank you once again, Poker Boy. Patty is waiting for you."

The guy in the golf outfit nodded as well and the next moment I was back in my office floating over Las Vegas.

And Patty was there.

She grabbed me and hugged me and then kissed me.

"You're alive and back here," she said, holding me at arm's length. "So I assume it worked."

"Laverne and some guy in golf clothes from the Time Board seem to think it did."

"Time Board?" Patty asked.

"Yeah, that's what I said."

I sure like the new duds," she said. "Brings back great memories."

I glanced down at the black suit, black tie, black vest, black slacks, and pure white, over-starched shirt. I also still had on the black Fedora.

"You want to help me out of them?" I asked. "No real air-conditioning back in those days."

"I remember," she said.

"You in Vegas at that time?" I asked. I knew she was at least that old, but no idea how old she really was.

"I was," she said, rubbing up against me as her uniform from the MGM Grand changed into a low-cut cigarette girl outfit with the Golden Gate logo on it.

"What?" I asked.

"I thought you were so handsome back then. I just stared at you all the time you were in there until you suddenly vanished. I wanted to help you out of that suit then. Been waiting seventy-two years for this fantasy to come true."

With that we went instantly from my office to our bedroom in Patty's apartment and she pushed me back on the bed and began peeling off the cigar girl costume as I sat there and watched until she was totally naked.

And then she stood me up, tossed my hat onto the bed, and slowly, oh, so slowly, worked to untie my tie.

That took an amazingly long time to do between kisses, but as I had learned tonight, time was very relative.

And the buttons on my vest took even longer.

Or it sure seemed that way. And I loved every moment of it.

ABOUT THE AUTHOR

Considered one of the most prolific writers working in modern fiction, *USA Today* bestselling writer Dean Wesley Smith published almost two hundred novels in forty years, and hundreds and hundreds of short stories across many genres.

At the moment he produces novels in several major series, including the time travel Thunder Mountain novels set in the Old West, the galaxy-spanning Seeders Universe series, the urban fantasy Ghost of a Chance series, a superhero series starring Poker Boy, and a mystery series featuring the retired detectives of the Cold Poker Gang.

His monthly magazine, *Smith's Monthly*, which consists of only his own fiction, premiered in October 2013 and offers readers more than 70,000 words per issue, including a new and original novel every month.

During his career, Dean also wrote a couple dozen *Star Trek* novels, the only two original *Men in Black* novels, Spider-Man and X-Men novels, plus novels set in gaming and television worlds. Writing with his wife Kristine Kathryn Rusch under the name Kathryn Wesley, he wrote the novel for the NBC miniseries The Tenth Kingdom and other books for *Hallmark Hall of Fame* movies.

He wrote novels under dozens of pen names in the worlds of comic books and movies, including novelizations of almost a dozen films, from *The Final Fantasy* to *Steel* to *Rundown*.

Dean also works as a fiction editor, starting at Pulphouse Publishing, then at *VB Tech Journal*, then Pocket Books. With

WMG Publishing, he edits two acclaimed anthology series: *Fiction River,* for which he acts as series editor with Kristine Kathryn Rusch, and the Hugo Award-winning *Pulphouse Fiction Magazine,* as well as a monthly magazine featuring all his own work called *Smith's Monthly.* And in 2022, he was named editor of *Writers of the Future.*

For more information about Dean's books and ongoing projects, please visit his website at www.deanwesleysmith.com and sign up for his newsletter.

ANGRY EARTH

LEAH R. CUTTER

San Francisco, March, 1906

Dang it! Where was that apothecary shop?

Annabella Lee walked up Post Street in San Francisco, circling back toward the Chinese neighborhood near Union Square. She must have walked past it. Probably while gawking at all the tall buildings. Or maybe the cable cars. Or even all the people!

The city was nothing at all like the quiet village of Modesto, where she'd grown up. It had taken them two days to travel by carriage, north to Stockton, then only a single day to ride the train into the city. Before the railroad had gone in, it would have taken five, maybe even seven days to travel by horseback to the city.

And all the wonders of the city! Those tall stone buildings! The elegantly dressed women, the fashionable men with their hats! How crowded the streets were, the hustle and bustle!

Annabella Lee now understood why Mistress had insisted on her wearing this tailored suit dress, done in a beautiful pastel blue, with a frilly white blouse. The entire outfit struck her as fussy, and it wouldn't last a day in the workshop, practicing spells and conjurations. However, she fit in better with the crowds here, being so dressed up.

At least it was 1906 now, and she wasn't required to wear some sort of ridiculous hoop skirt or petticoat! Or even a bustle. The late March weather still held a bite to it, and she was actually glad for the jacket she wore over the blouse. And for her solid boots, which weren't ladylike in the least. They better befit a country girl, like her.

"Can I help you, Miss?" a handsome man inquired as she gawked and gazed some more. He was tall and skinny as a young colt, with curly brown hair and a huge mustache that took up most of the bottom of his face. The dove gray suit he wore was perfectly tailored, and his black boots were well polished.

He looked like the perfect gentleman, if it weren't for his beady black eyes and lingering sneer.

"Oh, thank you, thank you! I'm looking for Fong's apothecary," Annabella Lee said as she fumbled out the address from her tiny hand purse.

What she carried in there was one of the reasons why Mistress had allowed Annabella Lee to go into the city on her own. In addition to the tiny Derringer handgun were two glass vials of knockout gas, along with a pinch of this and a dab of that, all easily combined into whatever spell Annabella Lee needed.

She might have had more than one such satchel of components sewn into the sleeves of her dress, and the waist of the lacy shirt, and even along the hem of her skirt.

Never knew what sort of trouble you might run into, particularly in such a wild place as the city.

"Ah, yes, Fong's," the young man said, nodding. "I can't accompany you the entire way, but I can at least point you in the right direction."

"Oh, thank you, thank you!" Annabella Lee said.

He gallantly offered her his elbow and off they went.

After about half an hour, during which Mr. Mitchell regaled her with tales of his train ride all the way across the country (!!!) Annabella Lee was certain she was even more lost than even. They'd turned down a poorer street, and the buildings were now poorly stacked brick, the streets closed in, and the people dressed in work clothes. However, most of the signs were in Chinese, so maybe they were going the right direction after all.

"Now," Mr. Mitchell said, patting her hand and then slipping his elbow away. "Fong's is just ahead. One and a half more blocks, then turn right, down the alley. The shop is on your left, with the bright red door. Can't miss it!" he promised her. He doffed his hat and gave her a slight bow before wheeling around and going back the way they'd come.

Annabella Lee didn't like the feel of this neighborhood. Not because it was poor—she'd seen poor, before. The families who all shared a single bed in a one-room house, never enough to eat and nothing to occupy the mind. Mistress brought food to the poorer families sometimes, tending to the little ones when they were sick, with her healing potions and spells.

No, there was something desperate and hard in the air, here. Something Annabella Lee had felt before, in other neighborhoods. A hunger that lingered, making the air sticky, filled with traces of rotting fruit.

When Annabella Lee had asked Mistress about it, the first time she'd felt it, Mistress had explained that the earth was angry here, for reasons she didn't fully comprehend. And that this was likely to be their last visit to the city for quite some time.

Annabella Lee had been disappointed, but hadn't pestered Mistress for more details as Mistress had also seemed perturbed by the notion.

The alley was right where Mr. Mitchell had said it was, and there was the red door as well. However, the door was locked and there was no sign that anyone had come this way in a while.

Disappointed, Annabella Lee turned around to leave, only to find that a young ruffian had snuck up behind her.

He had yellowed buck teeth and a long face, pale from a lack of sunshine. Greasy hair hung down over a broad forehead, partially covering wide, wild eyes. He wore a plain black jacket over even plainer black pants, with mere rags tied over his feet.

"Give us yer purse and ye won't be hurt. Much," he said with a leer as he reached out a dirty hand with ragged nails.

"No!" Annabella Lee said, darting to the side.

The young man reached out to snatch at her, barely missing her.

Annabella Lee collided with the ashbins she hadn't paid attention to, flailing but managing to keep on her feet.

The man stalked toward her. She was trapped, her back to the wall, the bins and other refuse blocking her path.

Dang it! She didn't have a spell prepared! She should have known, going into an alley like this, that anything could happen.

What spell could she do on the fly?

Then she realized what was blocking her.

Ashbins. Yes.

Mistress was going to be so angry with her for ruining her gloves. But it was for a good cause.

Annabella Lee ran her fingertips across the top of the soot-covered bin, gathering up as much of the ash as she could. Then, she quickly drew the sigil for a conjure air spell in front of her.

Normally, the component for this spell was the tufts of dandelion seeds. But really, anything that was light and floated easily would do.

Mistress didn't always approve of Annabella Lee's improvisations. Not using the precise ingredients sometimes led to unanticipated consequences.

But, needs must when the devil drives. Or something like that.

The sigil flashed with a dark red color, instead of the usual light yellow. Heated air exploded from Annabella Lee's palms, smelling of smoke, and sending the ruffian crashing into the far wall of the alley.

Without waiting to see what damage she'd done, Annabella Lee turned to hurry away.

Only to see Mr. Mitchell stepping out from the shadows, giving her a slow clap with his gloved hands.

Without waiting this time, Annabella Lee pulled out the

small Derringer pistol she carried in her purse and aimed it at the man. It fit comfortably in her hand, and had two silver bullets ready and loaded.

Mr. Mitchell stopped and gaped at her. "Really? You would shoot me? Just like that?"

Annabella Lee checked behind her quickly, but she didn't see anyone else sneaking up on her. "You'd send someone to mug me just like that," she said.

"Yes, but that was because I thought you were just a country hick," Mr. Mitchell admitted. "Not a seasoned spell caster." He gave her an evil smile. "No, I have better uses for you. For your blood, now."

"Good thing you're not getting any," Annabella Lee said.

"Now, my dear, you're not about to shoot anyone, so you might as well just come with me," Mr. Mitchell said.

Was that a dark red gleam he now had in his eyes?

"And go where?" Annabella Lee said, checking over her shoulder again, just in case this was a distraction and someone was coming up behind her.

Though the way Mr. Mitchell was looking so smugly at her, he appeared certain that he could take her on his own.

"The earth is hungry," Mr. Mitchell intoned, as if he was starting a bit of conjuration. "It needs the power and the blood. Can't you feel it?"

"Fool," Annabella Lee said. That was magic for simpletons. "Feed the earth blood and all it will want is more. Feed the earth peace and it will grow content."

"Feed the earth power and it will pay you back thrice-fold," Mr. Mitchell insisted.

"The earth is insatiable," Annabella Lee said slowly, as if talking to a simpleton. Which she obviously was. "It's so much bigger than you. It will take everything you have, and demand more. It's already angry."

If there was a coven of spell casters here in the city following such idiocy, no wonder the air in some of the neighborhoods felt so polluted!

"Which is why I intend to feed it you, and your power," Mr. Mitchell said, reaching out a hand, a small blue flame already coming to life in his palm.

Good thing Annabella Lee had the Derringer, and not a spell. Though she was experienced with magic, he was obviously much stronger.

Not strong enough to stop a bullet, though.

Annabella Lee aimed carefully and shot Mr. Mitchell through the heart. The gunshot made a quiet pop even in the confines of the alley, the recoil a hard push against her palm, the smell of gun powder quickly wafting away.

Mr. Mitchell staggered back, the look of surprise on his face comical in its extreme.

"You shot me!" he said as he dropped down to his knees.

Already, the silver was working its way into his bloodstream. He wasn't fully a demon, but only partially so. Maybe he'd merely made a pact with a creature of the netherworlds, instead of allowing one to ride his soul.

A dark hole began to open up underneath Mr. Mitchell, getting ready to swallow him. Probably something he'd prepared, only intending for it to be her body on the ground. The stench of rotten fruit belched out, and that sticky feeling of hunger swaddled her.

"Yes, I shot you," Annabella Lee said distinctly. "And good riddance."

As the body was already starting to disappear, she didn't bother wasting her second bullet.

Instead, she hurried away, putting her Derringer pistol back into her bag before she stepped out onto the brighter street.

While her gloves were ruined, only a bit of ash still clung to her dress. Hopefully, she'd be able to wash that out later.

No one would be able to trace the killing to her. There probably wouldn't even be a body to discover.

Not if the idiots were doing what she thought they were doing, feeding the insatiable earth blood and power.

Yes, Mistress was right. This might be the last time they could visit the city, if the ground under the city was this angry.

Annabella Lee walked up to the next major intersection, amazed to find that it was the street with Fong's Apothecary on it. Now, she just had to figure out which direction to go, pick up the supplies that she was supposed to acquire, and hurry back to the cottage where Mistress was staying.

She had news that wouldn't wait.

And they might have to shorten their stay in the city, before the earth lashed out, say, with an earthquake or something.

ABOUT THE AUTHOR

Leah R. Cutter writes page-turning fiction in exotic locations, such as a magical New Orleans, the ancient Orient, Hungary, the Oregon coast, rural Kentucky, Seattle, Minneapolis, and many others.

She writes literary, fantasy, mystery, science fiction, and horror fiction. Her short fiction has been published in magazines like Alfred Hitchcock's Mystery Magazine and Talebones, anthologies like Fiction River, and on the web. Her long fiction has been published both by New York publishers as well as small presses.

Find out more about Leah at:
www.LeahCutter.com

facebook.com/leah.cutter
bookbub.com/authors/leah-cutter

DESERT SCORPION

JASON A. ADAMS

Heat.

Heat is what defines the Sonoran Desert in summertime. Heat and lack of moisture.

A silvery sun cuts through the bone-dry atmosphere like a knife, roasting plant and animal alike. Sandstone outcrops painted yellow and red by the ages reflect the heat like rocks around a campfire. Temperatures hit upwards of a hundred and five in the air most days, even higher on the salty caliche surface. Saguaro cacti the color of gangrene stretch their arms toward the lapis-blue sky, and scrubby mesquite and palo verde trees crowd thickly around any spot that gathers the scant dew. The plants provide some shade, but only for critters built low to the ground.

Anything without stickers or stingers has a mighty rough time out on the pan.

Burt had neither.

He lay huddled in a small depression he'd manage to scrape out of the sun-baked dirt under an overhanging shelf of rock, waiting for the sun to finish its business and go to bed. He'd spent the last—seven nights? Eight?—stumbling through this God-rotted canyon, trying to get some sort of bearings. He wasn't making more than a mile or two a day, maybe less. Sleeping during the day and traveling at night had kept him alive so far, but only just.

Maybe alive enough to pay Ollie Swilling back. Him and his ranch hands and vaqueros.

The nights were just as dry as the days, if cooler.

The sunlight went out like God snuffed his candle. With no clouds and no water in the air, dusk wasn't much out here.

Burt staggered to his feet, his blue cotton shirt lined with salty white streaks, his trousers stiff with sweat and grime. He hoped to find a barrel cactus or some other source of water. Not that he was thirsty any more, or hungry for that matter.

Not a good sign, but he still lived.

Finally, he carved into a fat saguaro and pulled out a chunk of damp flesh. At least he still had his knife. His .44 still hung in the worn leather holster tied down on his right hip, but he had no powder or bullets. The heavy dragoon might do for a club, if he managed to sneak up on something.

Burt slowly chewed the nasty mess as he started the next leg of his never-ending trudge, hating the bitter taste but knowing it bought him a few more hours. Maybe he'd find something dead that the buzzards and coyotes hadn't got to yet.

Maybe something would find him. Scorpions, with any luck. He reckoned he was still fast and steady enough to get one of the little monsters before it got him. They tasted worse than cactus, but at this point he wasn't picky.

Coyotes yipped and yapped in the distance. Desert owls flew past on silent wings. Unseen things scrabbled through the pebbles and scree.

Burt made more noise than the rest of the animals put together.

His breathing loud and ragged, his feet kicking rocks and crushing sticks, his occasional groan as he crested a hill only to see more of the same stretching out in the moonlight. He was a regular one-man band.

A cruel mesquite root caught his foot and he went down. Rolling over on his back, the stored heat of the day uncomfortable against the chafed skin where his shirt rode up, he stared upward and outward, marveling at all the light in the sky. People talked of the blackness of night, but he couldn't see a single speck of it. Stars filled the heavens from one horizon to the other. There was the big hunter. Over yonder what looked like a scorpion, long tail and all.

All that beautiful light...

Burt shook himself, catching the oncoming crazy before it

took hold. He rolled onto his belly, came up on hands and knees —and went down again. He wondered hazily if this was the last time.

The ground trembled beneath him. Or was that his soul trying to get out of the husk that trapped it?

Noises. A musky smell of horseflesh.

Voices...voices in some other language. Angels?

He peeled one dry, bloodshot eye and rolled it upward. A circle of horses ringed him, holding up feathered and painted Papago braves.

"Go away," he tried to say. He couldn't tell if he spoke aloud or not.

Above him, the Indians looked at each other, babbling in their savage language. Finally, the biggest brave swung down off his horse. He knelt, gathered what was left of Burt in his arms, draped him over his pony's rump, and the group began walking toward a low ridge in the distance.

What the hell. Might as well get a nap in before the Indians did whatever they were gonna do.

Burt closed his eyes and let Brother Pony rock him to sleep.

～

FEELING BETRAYED, Burt came back to consciousness when he hit the ground. A gabble of voices surrounded him; men, women, and children. He scrabbled through last night, finally remembering the Papago braves and the horse ride. No breeze across the top of his head, so Burt still had his hair. Hands and feet weren't tied, either. Coarse fur and the rank, garbagey smell that never quite went away told Burt he was laid out on a bearskin.

Pretty strange treatment for a white captive, but he'd heard the Papago were different.

Mesquite smoke drifted through his nostrils, along with a

whiff of roasting venison that set his stomach to grumbling. He didn't have enough wet inside for his mouth to water.

He might not be tied, but Burt saw no reason to take chances. He snuck his eyes open a tiny crack.

And jumped like a jackrabbit. All he could see was a big Papago buck's face, cheeks streaked with white and yellow.

The face pulled back as the other Papago burst out laughing. His place was taken by an older man, this one without paint and sporting long gray hair.

The elder wore a knee-length tunic of pale deerskin suede, over side-stitched buckskin trousers. Long leather mocs covered his feet, with the bent-over rawhide flap on the toes that marked him as primarily a walker, not a rider.

Kicking a jumping or barrel cactus wasn't any fun.

Burt sat up, crossed his legs, and laid his hands on his knees, palm up. He was in a domed hut made of bentwood poles and covered with hides and woven grass. What the locals called a *wickiup*.

"*¿Tienes sed?*" asked the elder in passable Spanish.

"Um. *Si.* Yes. *¿Agua, por favor?*"

The old man rattled something in Papago and a pretty young thing brought a skin bag heavy with wonderful, beautiful water. She held the horn spout to his lips, and he drank a little, swishing the water around, wetting his cracked and burnt lips. Best not to drink much, yet. Give his dried-out flesh a little time to soak it in.

One more swallow wouldn't hurt, he supposed.

"I am called Running Fox. You are a white man, yes?" he asked, voice heavily accented but clear. "From the sun's roasting, it is hard to tell."

"I'm sure glad you habla English," Burt said, wincing as his voice creaked and croaked past his parched voice box. "Yessir. I'm Sergeant Burton Jennings. Call me Burt. From MacIntyre's

Rifles, U.S. First Dragoons. Down here scouting out the territory we're fixin' to buy from Mexico."

"It appears to me that you are here feeding yourself to the desert." Running Fox said. "You are cavalry, yet you have no horse, no sword, and no rifle."

"I did have all those, sir. I lost them when Ollie Swilling and his boys bushwhacked me." Burt coughed, took another tiny sip from the waterskin.

"Oliver Swilling, the cattle man? The one who is trying to claim all the wild cattle?" Running Fox's expression didn't change, but he leaned forward hands on his knees and eyes shining like a newly minted silver dollar.

"That's him," Burt said. "See, he knows if Ambassador Gadsden gets Santa Anna to sign this treaty they're working up, all this land becomes part of the New Mexico Territory. And then here come the homesteaders, cavalry, and lawmen. That won't do for him, not at all."

Running Fox rocked back on his haunches, studying Burt.

"This Oliver Swilling preys on the Desert People as well," he said, voice like the edge of freshly napped flint. "He rubs out our men. Steals our women. Even the children. I would do much to rid the desert of this demon."

He shook his head like a man who knows he's woolgathering, then sat forward again and tapped Burt's knee with a gnarled finger.

"And what do *you* wish to do, Sergeant Burton Jennings?"

"I need to get back on a horse, and get after Swilling. If he keeps taking out us scouts, won't nobody know what's what. Besides..." Burt paused for another sip of water, smiling at the Papago girl. She smiled back, deep dimples in her cheeks.

"Besides, Ollie's supplyin' all the Mexicans and renegade Apache he can find with rifles, powder, and shot. He wants to make the whole blasted desert into a killin' floor. While everyone's distracted, he'll do as he pleases."

"I have seen trouble in my dreams," Running Fox said, looking toward the wickiup's curved ceiling. "And I have seen *you*, Burton Jennings."

"*Me*? What do you mean, me?"

Running Fox smiled and patted Burt's knee.

"I'm sure it is nothing. You will help us or you will not. We will certainly help *you*, for that is what friends do. For now, you must eat. Drink more water. Rest and heal."

The other Papago, who had been watching the whole conversation, now broke up. Some brought in hides piled with steaming ribs and joints of muley deer. Others brought in gourds and clay jugs filled with water, corn beer, and some sort of sweet, syrupy wine.

"Come, my new friend," Running Fox said, taking a jug and trading it for the pretty girl's waterskin. "Drink the *tiswin*. You will be back to yourself very soon. Wind-in-the-Leaves, take care of our guest."

She smiled again, and scooted to sit beside Burt, her soft hip against his as she offered him a jug that gave off the sweet smell of the sweetest new cactus jelly and made his eyes burn like the rawest new whiskey. Her hair smelled of mesquite and warm woman. Burt found his arm around her waist, somehow.

"Pleased to meet you, ma'am. Reckon I'll just call you Wind, if you don't care."

What the hell? After the week he'd had, Burt could sure use a drink or two.

∼

TIME AND PEOPLE whirled around Burt.

Faces came into focus and whipped away, laughing or shouting.

Gourds and jugs were held to his mouth, and Burt drank.

Hands stripped away his shirt and trousers. Smeared him with muddy clay. The clay held the eye-watering stink of creosote and desert mustard.

Burt coughed. Vomited.

Laughter around him. Claps on the back.

More tiswin. More words and sights he couldn't understand.

Running Fox chanted and the braves and squaws answered.

Burt lay on his back. Wind-in-the-Leaves straddled him. Rode him.

Cheering men and women.

Sparks. Darkness.

Sleep.

~

SUNLIGHT FELL across Burt's face, waking him. He sat up, stretched. Felt beside him for Wind-in-the-Leaves. Nothing there.

He opened his eyes.

Burt was still in the wickiup, but he was it, as far as people went. All the blankets and most of the gourds, jugs, and baskets were gone.

A few wisps of smoke still idled up from the firepit, lazily curling up toward a smoke hole, past a rack made of sticks and thongs which held his clothing. It had all been washed, and his gunbelt and boots oiled. On the floor beside the rack, two small pouches held bullets and powder, and a wooden box with Spanish markings held percussion caps. Burt's pistol was loaded, with two more cylinders in the belt loops.

Hm. And a fine morning to *you*, Running Fox.

Burt dressed, realizing most of the pain from sore muscles and sunburnt hide had left him. He felt more like a human being than he had in days.

The only mirror he could find was his knife blade, which had also been oiled and honed to a far finer edge than he could manage himself. Hard to tell in such a poor reflection, but Burt could swear the burn was almost gone.

He checked his gun, rotating the cylinder and working the action. It hadn't suffered from the desert near as much as he had, thank goodness.

It had work to do, after all.

At the wickiup's door, Burt found a full waterskin, along with a leather pouch containing pemmican and jerky. Gratitude swelled inside him toward these so-called savages who'd treated him far better than the last white men he'd run across.

He slung the waterskin and food pouch over his shoulder and stepped outside. The day was already hot and dry, but not quite to the hide-for-your-life stage.

The wickiup sat by itself at the base of a mesa. The surrounding area showed some traces of humans, but the ground had been combed and strewn with rocks, sticks, and other debris as only Indians could. He knew people had been here, but no idea how many, or where they'd gone.

He looked east, then south.

He turned to the west and nearly filled his britches.

Running Fox stood calmly, hands behind his back, smiling serenely. Wind-in-the-Leaves stood beside him, her own demure smile full of knowledge. She came forward and touched his hand.

"I'm glad you are awake, Burton Jennings," Running Fox said. "For three days, all you have done is drink the tiswin and dream." His gaze flicked to Wind-in-the-Leaves and back to Burt. "Well, perhaps you have done more than that."

"Uh, I was a little drunk. I mean, I'm sorry." Burt felt the heat rising up his face.

Running Fox said something to Wind and she laughed, a merry tinkling sound like water in an arroyo after the rains.

"Do not worry, my young friend," Running Fox said. "Among us, there is no shame in celebrating each other. Besides, she tells me you leave our people with a great gift."

"Gift?" Burt said, eyebrows high. "I didn't leave..." He broke off when he saw how Wind rubbed her belly.

Oh. That kind of gift.

"Listen," he said. "I'm glad to make an honest woman of Wind, and to take care of her and the child. But right now..."

"Right now you must go stop an evil man from making all of the people of the Sonora suffer," Running Fox said. He spoke to Wind again, and she dashed off behind a large fan of scree, returning a few minutes later leading a dappled, thick-legged, sturdy-bodied pony. No saddle, but at least it wore a blanket and had a braided leather bridle.

"Ride south from moonrise to set, then half a sun," Running Fox said. "Look for the place where a big yellow rock sits on a red one. You should find the tracks of the men you seek."

"Good," Burt said, his hand dropping to the butt of his pistol. "Me'n Sam Colt have a few things to say to him."

"No. You must not use your gun," Running Fox said. "That will only look like a murder to your people and to the Mexicans. More trouble will come, for you and maybe for us as well, not less."

"So what do you want me to do?" Burt asked. "Want me to ask him to say he's sorry? Pick up his mess and go home?"

"Take this," Running Fox said, handing a strip of something dried and lumpy to Burt.

A scorpion tail.

"I don't reckon I can sting him with this," Burt said, trying to keep the meanness out of his voice. "Even if I got close enough, there ain't any juice left."

"In your dreams, you spoke of Brother Scorpion," Running Fox said. "Do you remember?"

Burt *did* remember. He'd seen the chittering bodies scurrying across the desert floor, growing larger as they moved. He remembered seeing one in the stars. How he'd hoped to catch one so he could eat.

He looked at Running Fox, but couldn't find any words.

"Yes, Burton Jennings," Running Fox said. "I too have seen the scorpion. He is the spirit of change. Of Chaos which turns into Order. He is also the spirit of strength. Brother Scorpion watches you, and you will use *his* power to defeat the war-talkers, child-killers, and animal stealers."

"How can I do that?" Burt asked, trying to push the mummified stinger back. "I don't know anything about your Indian hoodoo."

"You don't need our medicine, Burton. You have enough of your own. More than two bands of Papago. How else could you survive with no food or water in a land which kills at a whim?"

He had magic? This was all crazy!

"Help me out, here. What can I do with a dried-up scorpion tail against five or six armed men?"

"Listen to me, Burton Jennings. You must learn these words and when to say them. The power will go through you, but you have not learned how to talk to Brother Scorpion yourself. Not yet."

Burt shivered at that *not yet,* but he listened anyway.

∽

A DAY AND A HALF LATER, Burt left his pony staked near a patch of sagebrush and crept up over a small hill. Down below, casting a long dark shadow in the sun's last hurrah of the evening, stood a low adobe rancho, surrounded by pinyon-pine stockades and corrals.

The enclosures barely held all the wild cattle and mustangs Ollie and his boys had been rounding up.

Damn. The walls of the rancho had to be two feet thick. Heavy slab shutters with firing crosses covered every window, and the door looked stout enough to stop a cannon shot.

Time to see of old Running Fox was a shaman or a shyster.

Burt waited for two hours or more. Waited until the sun finished going to bed and the last bit of lamplight went out behind the windows. Then he waited a bit longer, just because.

Finally, when he could hear grunting, snuffling snores even as far away as he was, Burt crept down the hill.

On his belly, he snaked his way toward the rancho, inching along on toes and fingertips.

Ten feet from the house, Burt stopped, pulled the scorpion tail from his breast pocket, and tossed it right in front of the porch steps.

Then he hightailed it back to his watching spot.

When he got there, the moon had risen, full and bright. The entire front of the rancho was bathed in silvery light.

Burt stood and shouted toward the moon in words he didn't understand and could barely pronounce, full of clicks and stops.

Running Fox had told him the meaning, though.

Brother Scorpion! Come to the aid of those your people. Come to the pain of those who threaten your lands. Come as I call, Brother Scorpion.

There was more, but Running Fox told him that was the gist.

At first, nothing happened.

Of course it didn't. Indians didn't have any more magic than—

Something scuttled across Burt's foot.

Then something else.

He looked down and saw a dozen multi-legged, curve-tailed terrors scurrying down the hill.

In the moonlight, the desert floor looked like the sea.

Waves and tides of pincered bodies surged toward the rancho.

Scorpions the size of his hand, all the way down to the little bark scorpions.

The tiny, far more dangerous ones, shorter than his little finger and like to make a man puke himself to death with nothing more than a scratch from the evil barb riding high over their backs.

The scorpions swarmed up the porch.

Up the walls.

Under the door and through the window slits.

Inside the rancho, someone hollered. Then screamed.

More screams followed.

The door flew open.

A man-sized creature formed of scorpions staggered out.

Fell down the steps.

Eventually, all the screaming stopped.

Burt stood, mouth hanging open and ice running through his veins.

A rare cloud passed over the moon, casting the ground below in shadow. When the cloud retreated, the scorpions were gone.

Burt started down the hill, flinching as one last chitinous body darted across his path. He found something vaguely Ollie-shaped, though from the swollen and purpled face, it was hard to be sure.

Inside the rancho, he found five other bodies. Plus several cases of cheap rifles and ammunition, and a strongbox filled to bursting with gold and silver dollars and pesos.

And a ledger with all the names of the business owners, ranchers, and others who he'd been working with.

Everything the territorial and Mexican lawmen would need.

Thank you, Running Fox and Brother Scorpion!

∼

Six months later, Burt stood in parade formation with Captain MacIntyre and the rest of the rifle company at the Tucson depot as Ambassador Gadsden stepped down from a stagecoach draped with red, white, and blue bunting.

The treaty of purchase had been ratified, transferring the La Mesilla area from Mexico to the New Mexico Territory.

The Washington starched-shirts would get all the reward and all the credit, but Burt and the rest of MacIntyre's boys were the ones who'd done all the work to expand this little corner of the growing Union.

Burt thought he might leave the Army now that his job was done. Talk of secessions and other such hooraw back east, not to mention a certain Papago lady with a bun in the oven, led him to believe he might make a pretty good farmer or rancher.

Plus, he needed to spend some more time talking to Running Fox. And maybe to Brother Scorpion.

Maybe he'd make something more than a farmer or rancher before they fed his carcass to a dry, desert hole, which hopefully was way on down the rails when he couldn't ride nor walk anymore.

ABOUT THE AUTHOR

Jason A. Adams writes across the spectrum. His stories include science fiction, fantasy, horror, Appalachian folk tales, romance, and other genres. Often blended together.

You can also find his stories in the pages of *Pulphouse Magazine, Mystery, Crime, and Mayhem,* and the Winter Holiday Spectaculars from WMG Publishing. Several more stories are pending publication in various productions, so stay tuned!

Jason, a recovering Air Force brat who grew up all over the US and Japan, now perches in the mountains of Southwest Virginia with his beautiful wife Kari Kilgore, three spoiled cats, and assorted wild visitors from the nearby forest.

You can find more of his work and sign up for updates from the Brain Squirrels at
www.jasonadams.info

EMBRACING THE FLAMES

DAYLE A. DERMATIS

I.

Mae's mother died when Mae was eight years old.

The evening after she was laid to rest in River View Cemetery, Mae eased out of her bed and past her sleeping nanny, and made her way down the two flights of stairs. Her fingers slipped from one hand-carved baluster to the next, touching the ornate bumps of cinnamon-colored wood, the same wood that made up the beadboard along the wall, and the stairs themselves, and indeed most of the house.

Then she padded across the cold foyer in her bare feet, wearing only a lace-edged, white linen nightgown, her hair in plaits for sleeping, to her father's study.

She'd loved her mother very much, and her stomach was twisted and aching from sadness.

She barely knew her father, a man who seemed impossibly large, with mutton chops that framed a mouth that she'd never seen smile. She knew he was an important man—a lumber man—and that they lived in their big house with a tower on the outskirts of Portland, Oregon, because of his business.

Even still, she loved him, and although she loved her nanny, too, in a different way, right now she needed the comfort of family.

She crept up to the doorway and peered around it.

The beadboard and picture rail were the same warm cinnamon-colored wood as the rest of the house, and the walls were painted a dark red above, the color of the wine her parents sometimes drank with dinner. Bookcases filled with leather-bound books lined the room, the gaslight reflecting off the glass fronts.

Her father sat in an armchair by the fireplace, not at his desk. He'd loosened his tie and unbuttoned his coat. Mae had never seen him like that before. The fire had burned down, sending more pungent smoke into the air than heat, but he didn't look as if he'd called for someone to stoke it. He had a glass tumbler in his left hand, a half inch of reddish-gold liquid in the bottom. From the amount left in the crystal bottle on the small pie table next to his chair, she guessed it hadn't been his first drink.

His right elbow was on the chair arm, his thumb and forefinger pressed against his nose.

Mae took a few steps into the room, then stopped, suddenly nervous. "Papa?"

He started, looked over at her. "Mae? What are you doing up? Where's Nanny?"

He didn't seem angry, so she crossed the room to stand next to his chair.

His eyes were red, and his breath smelled sharp, unpleasant.

"I miss Mama," she said.

She couldn't remember a time when she'd seen her father smile. Now, the edges of his mouth turned up beneath his thick mustache, but it felt sad. He rested a large hand on her shoulder; the weight of it surprised her.

"I miss her, too, Mae."

He didn't say anything else. He took a long swallow of his drink, and after a moment, he seemed to have forgotten Mae was there. A mostly burned log in the fireplace collapsed with a shush and crackle of sparks. The clock on the desk ticked.

Mae felt tears crowd into her throat. She wanted to crawl into her Papa's lap, feel his arms around her, feel the warmth of the fire. She couldn't stand the near-silence anymore, so she asked the first question that came to mind.

"Papa? Why wasn't Mama's friend at the...funeral?"

He turned back to her. "Which friend, Mae? I thought all of her friends were there."

Mae recognized some of Mama's lady friends from the funeral. When Mama would have them over for tea, Mae would sit at the top of the stairs, her face pressed against the balusters, to admire their pretty dresses and hats. But she wasn't talking about any of those.

"The tall man," she said.

Papa set down the glass so hard, the liquid left inside almost sloshed out. "What tall man?"

He was hard to describe. Mae had seen him many times, and he looked like an angel: tall and slender, graceful, with a face that was both beautiful and frightening. He didn't have wings, though, and he wore normal clothes, so Mae didn't think he *was* an angel.

Papa looked angry, and Mae was afraid he was angry with her. She stumbled over her words. "In Mama's b-b-bedroom."

Now Papa's face flushed red. "In her *bedroom*?" His fingers clenched on Mae's shoulder, and she winced. She wanted to run away, run back up to her room and dive under the warm covers and pull them over her head.

"What were they doing?" Papa demanded.

"Just...talking," Mae squeaked. "When I came in, he would go away."

She could never explain *how* he went away; he didn't walk past her to the door, or through the door that led from Mama's sitting room to Papa's room. She tried to say that the man was really usually in Mama's sitting room, where Mama had all her papers and books and special things, because somehow she could tell that the man being in Mama's bedroom was a bad thing, but she couldn't get the words past her throat.

Papa yanked on the gold tasseled bell pull on the wall, which would summon their butler, Mr. Harrington.

What followed after that was a frightening flurry of activity and noise. Papa refilled his glass, drank it all down, and threw the glass into the fireplace, where it shattered. Blue flames leapt up to lick at the alcohol. Mae clapped her hands over her ears.

When Mr. Harrington arrived, Papa shouted at him to get all the servants. Some of them, like Nanny, had already gone to bed, and assembled in the drawing room half-dressed. Nanny found Mae crouched by the fireplace in Papa's study, but Papa wouldn't let Nanny take Mae back upstairs. Nanny had to stand with the rest of them: Mr. Harrington, the cook, the two maids, two footmen, the gardener and handyman, the driver of the sleek black car that Mae had ridden in several times.

Nanny stood with her hands on Mae's shoulders, pulling Mae as close against her as she could, as Papa paced and ranted, his face red and his voice sometimes stumbling.

He demanded to know who else had seen the man. No one had. He shouted at each one, accused them of lying, but they insisted. One of the maids was crying. Mr. Harrington finally stepped forward and spoke in careful, measured words, respect in his deep voice, appealing to father's sense of reason.

It did no good. Papa shouted for a steamer trunk to be brought to Mama's bedroom, and for a fire to be built. There was confusion as the handyman went to find the trunk, and the footmen went to start the fire, and the maids were unsure what to do until Mr. Harrington sent them back to bed. Papa storming back into his study and came out with the crystal bottle of whiskey before stomping up the stairs.

Nanny took Mae upstairs, but Mae refused to go to her own room. She ran away from Nanny and hid behind one of the long, dusty rose brocade curtains, peering out. Her heart pounded and her stomach hurt, but she needed to see what Papa was going to do.

Mae had always loved Mama's bedroom, with its rose-sprigged wallpaper and the long curtains. Because it was at the corner of the house, there were windows on two walls, flooding the room with light during the day Everything was suffused with Mama's smell; her favorite scent was, unsurprisingly, roses. The four-poster bed with its barley-twist posts and many feather pillows, where Mama would cuddle with Mae on rainy days and tell her stories.

She didn't want Papa to touch anything. Mama was never coming back, Mae was old enough to understand that, but she still wanted everything to stay the same, from the pins Mama had dropped when she was putting on her hat that last morning, to the half-written letter on her sitting room desk.

The handyman brought the trunk into the room and left quickly. All the other servants had fled. Papa had stopped shouting, but he'd thrown off his jacket, and his broad shoulders were tight. Mae pressed her hands to her mouth as he opened Mama's wardrobe and threw all of her pretty dresses and skirts into the trunk. He didn't fold them, just grabbed them by the armful and tossed them in. Her hats, her shoes, and then he went to her dresser, where satin gloves and silk underthings followed.

At her dressing table, he swept all of her jewelry into the trunk.

He picked up the silver-backed mirror hair brush, with which Mama had brushed her hair, a hundred strokes every night, and often Mae's too. The brush and mirror had been Mama's grandmother's, she'd told Mae, and someday they would be Mae's.

Papa threw them into the trunk.

Mae's heart constricted, but she knew not to contradict or question Papa, even though she didn't understand why he was doing what he was doing.

The powders and perfume bottles Papa threw into the now-crackling fire. Mae winced as the glass shattered. Sweet rose mixed with acrid chemicals.

Then Papa went into Mama's sitting room. He came out with a large handful of papers and added them to the fire. The flames licked greedily at them. He paused to take a drink directly from the bottle he'd brought from downstairs. The stopper bounced on the carpet and then rolled under the dressing table. He didn't seem to notice, or care.

Mae was distressed about the brush and mirror, but her heart felt squeezed by a fist when she saw what he carried on his final trip out of the sitting room.

Mama's special book.

Mae knew this book was old and special. It was Mama's most important book, and she'd told Mae that when Mae was older, she'd explain what was in it, and teach Mae many special things.

The brown leather was worn and scuffed, and had none of the gold lettering that many book covers did. The paper had darkened with age, and the edges were rough and uneven.

"No," Mae said, but no sound came out.

Papa didn't even look at the book. He just threw it into the fireplace on top of everything else. The flames wrapped around it.

A whimper escaped Mae's throat, threatening to rise into a wail.

"Go," said a voice. She recognized its honeyed tone: the man Mama had talked with. "No one will see you."

A tingle washed down from her head to her toes, like she was being warmed by sunlight, only inside. It made no sense, but she believed the voice, believed that her father wouldn't notice what she was doing.

She *felt* invisible.

She darted out from behind the curtain, fell to her knees on the bottle-green–tiled hearth just in front of the brass andirons.

Behind her, her father slammed the trunk shut. For a moment, silence, and then a scrape as he grabbed the crystal bottle. A few short steps past where Mae knelt, and he was out of the room, turning the key on the gas light by the door before he slammed the door behind him.

Pushing the long sleeves of her nightgown back, Mae reached in with both hands and grabbed the book. She didn't wonder why the fire didn't hurt her hands. She simply knew it wouldn't.

The book was charred, sparks still glowing on the leather. She patted them out. They didn't leave blisters. She opened the book. Some of the pages had burned half away; others were smeared with sooty smoke. A tear escaped and rolled down Mae's cheek.

She couldn't read the book, but she had saved it. It was the only thing of her mother's she had left.

Mae climbed up onto her mother's high, wide bed. She slid the book beneath the pillows, then lay down. With one hand tucked beneath, her fingers grazing the edge of the book, she fell asleep.

She half-woke when she heard the door open and Nanny's voice saying, "I found her."

"Thank goodness," her father said. His hands were gentle as he scooped her up. Neither he nor Nanny said anything about the book, and then she heard the door to Mama's room close. They hadn't found it.

The wool of Papa's vest was scratchy against her cheek, and he still smelled of whisky.

Whatever had upset him so, at least he wasn't angry at Mae.

∼

THE NEXT MORNING, while her nanny was visiting the water closet, Mae snuck back into her mother's room and retrieved the book. The smell of smoke brought back all the memories of the night before.

She had a jewelry box, not as fancy as her mother's, which was covered in claret velvet. Mae's was a wooden box, mahogany, with her initials on a brass plate on the top. She had very little jewelry; she was too young to have expensive pieces. The box was the perfect size for the book.

She locked the box, put it back in her dressing table drawer, and looked around the room for a hiding place for the key. In the end, she tucked it inside her dress, the metal warming beneath her corset.

She heard a noise outside and climbed onto her cushioned window seat to look.

Below, she saw the handyman load the trunk onto the back of their motorcar. When it was strapped down, he tapped the side of the car to indicate he was done, and the driver pulled away.

Everything of Mama's was gone, except for the book.

And, she assumed, the man.

II.

Mae was thirteen before she was old enough to finally, truly understood why her father had flown into such a rage that night—the thought that his beloved wife had been unfaithful. Since then, he had withdrawn. Alcohol was his only solace, it seemed. Not so much that he didn't continue to be successful with his lumber business, but he never showed a temper again, and he was always gentle and kind with Mae. She saw more of him than she had before, although he still kept long hours.

That wasn't the only thing that happened the year she was thirteen.

Nanny was getting on in years—she hadn't been young when Mae's parents had hired her—and she wasn't as steady on her feet.

Thankfully Mae was in the room when Nanny stumbled on the edge of the hearth. The maid had just removed the peacock-shaped bronze fire screen to add some wood, so Nanny's skirt got closer to the flames than it should just as the half-burned logs in the fireplace shifted, sending sparks into the air.

Some of them landed on Nanny's black dress and white

apron. Neither of them noticed at first, Nanny because of her failing eyesight and Mae because she was reading.

But then Mae smelled a scent like burning leaves, and Nanny cried out.

Nanny waved her skirt and apron to put out the fire, but that just made the glowing embers flare up.

"Stop!" Mae cried. She fell to her knees and patted out the flames. Nanny's apron had large, singe-ringed holes in it, and her dress had a few, too. When Mae tugged on the hem, Nanny hissed in pain, and Mae saw that some of the embers had made it through her left stocking, too. The skin beneath was red and angry.

The maid came back with some firewood, and stopped when she saw what had happened.

"Cora, could you please get some salve and a clean bandage?" Mae asked. The young woman nodded, deposited the wood beside the fireplace, and hurried off.

"It doesn't look too bad," Mae said. "I don't think we'll need to call Dr. Wyatt."

"But Mae, your hands!" Nanny said. "You must have gotten burned, too."

Mae hadn't even thought about it. She turned her hands palm up. There was a bit of soot on them, but otherwise, the pale flesh was unmarred.

Nanny grabbed her wrists and pulled her hands closer to inspect them. Her brown eyes grew wide. "But there's not a mark on you..."

"I worked quickly," Mae said. "I barely touched anything before the flames were out."

But Nanny wasn't convinced. Not now, as Mae bandaged her leg, and not the next day, when she told Mae it was time for her to go.

Mae begged her to stay, but Nanny sighed, and the sound

pierced Mae's heart. She knew what it meant: there was no changing Nanny's mind.

After her nanny left, Mae begged her father for a governess who could teach her, or even better, a tutor. She was had already outstripped Nanny's knowledge, and her own thirst for learning burned like an ember inside her.

Her father indulged her. Despite his feelings for his late wife and her apparent betrayal, he never turned that hurt or anger onto his daughter. She had been, from the moment she was born, the apple of his eye, and he had seen both her intelligence and maturity growing in the past years. Understanding her need for freedom, he chose instead of a governess a lady's maid, and found a suitable tutor to educate her in a variety of subjects.

Although she was drawn to sums and numbers, and was more than competent with her writing the sciences, Mae had been given a love of reading from her mother.

Fairytales and fanciful stories. She would curl up against her mother side while her mother read to her in her beautiful, melodious voice, the stories by Grimm and *La Belle et la Bête* and more.

Her mother also told stories that Mae couldn't find in any book in the house or bookstore, no matter how diligently she searched. Stories of magic and wonder, and the premise that witches were not warty hags who ate children or prophesied doom, but were woman who did good in the world, healing and helping.

Now, late at night, when she was sure the rest of the household was asleep, Mae would collect her mother's old book from its hiding place.

Although she would've loved to keep it tucked under her pillow, comforted by the knowledge it rested below her head, she knew that wasn't a safe place. Even putting it under her mattress meant she would have to move it twice a year when the maids stripped the bed apart to air it out. Her jewelry box was not much better for a longer term solution.

The safest place to hide it, she realized, was in her mother's rooms.

They had been closed off after her mother's death, after her father had sent all of her mother's belongings away. A fine layer of dust coated the furniture, and half-burned logs still sat cold in the fireplace.

Once, as a very young child, Mae had been sitting near her mother's feet and tapping on the floor and objects around her. A section of the beadboard had moved slightly, and her mother had distracted her away from the section of wall. Mae had been too young to think of it again.

But when she had the book in hand after her mother's death, something made her remember that moment, and she crept in to discover there was a space behind the cinnamon-colored wooden beadboard.

A space that the book fit into perfectly, as if it had always belong there.

So now, she would go into her mother's room sitting room, retrieve the book from its hiding place, and return her own room. Sitting next to the fire, or in the summer close to a gas lamp, the flames' flickering a comfort that she couldn't explain, she would open the book on her lap slowly, reverently.

The cover was burgundy leather, long scratched and scuffed, with no title or other words. When she opened the book, the vanilla scent of old paper made her feel nostalgic for something she didn't know she missed.

On the first page was a list names. All women. The last name was her mother's.

No matter how many times she studied the book, studied the writing, she couldn't quite understand it. She felt as though she was on the cusp of understanding, so close she could taste it, but she never quite could.

It seemed to be in a language that didn't exist. Somehow she knew never to show the book to her father or to her nanny or to her tutor.

Still, there were many nights when she tried to read the book, gently tracing her fingertips across the words she felt she should understand. The handwriting changed periodically, and she could match each section to one of the women listed in the front by comparing the handwriting.

The only word she could read in the entire book was on the final page with writing on it. Enscribed by her mother.

Her own name. The last thing her mother had written was "Mae."

III.

When Mae was fifteen years old, she again saw the man she had spied in her mother's sitting room.

When she wasn't studying, she often found herself gazing into the flames of the nearest fireplace or gas lamp. She wasn't sure why, but the flickers endless undulating shapes fascinated her, drew her, almost hypnotized her.

When she was feeling fanciful, she imagined she could see shapes in the glowing crimson and orange and yellow movement. Shapes she couldn't always put a name to, but beings nonetheless.

She did read about fire salamanders and other such mythical creatures, and although she felt a tug of familiarity, she wouldn't swear she that was what she saw. One evening, she was curled on the settee in her own drawing room when the flames in her fireplace shifted and coalesced before her half-lidded, unfocused gaze.

At first she thought she had briefly nodded off, and even sharply pinched the skin of her forearm between her fingers because she was certain she was dreaming.

For out of the flames—or maybe it was a part of the flames

shifting—came the man she had seen in her mother's sitting room. The man she had told her father about. The man who had sent her father into rage and despair.

His hair was the unique golden hue of fire, and his clothes seem to shift between red and orange like the flicker of a flame. She had seen taffeta that did that, that tricked the eye, looking peacock blue from one angle and emerald from another, and almost iris purple from yet another, shifting between the colors as the skirt swished.

Other than the unusual hue, his clothing was no different than any other gentleman's of the day. His hair might have brushed a little long against his collar, and his cheekbones might have been unusually sharp, which a less observant person might not have noticed.

But Mae noticed.

She stood, straightened her back even though her corset already kept her posture firm, and said, "It is unseemly for an unmarried woman to have a man in her private rooms. Get out."

He took a step back, his eyes widening in surprise. "I mean you no harm," he said. "Quite the opposite, I—"

"I don't care what you have to say," Mae said. She was surprised to realize that was a lie. She remembered the sound of the voice and the warmth she'd felt. Even now, she felt some sort of pull towards the man, some kind of comfortable familiarity. No, more than that—almost as if he filled a hole she didn't know existed, slotting in next to her as if they were adjoining puzzle pieces.

It wasn't attraction, not how she understood it, anyway. She didn't want him to kiss her, didn't feel any of the things the women in books she shouldn't read (but did anyway, because there was no one to stop her) when they swooned and fluttered and yearned.

This was different.

She wanted it, but she didn't want it, because she had seen what had happened with her mother.

"I don't know why you were with my mother, but that knowledge has brought nothing but pain to our house. It shattered my father, made him question his love for my mother."

The man still looked unsettled. "But he shouldn't have known. He couldn't have."

Mae hung her head, the guilt rushing back. "I saw you, when I was too young to understand, and I told him after Mama died."

"Your mother and I...we didn't have that kind of relationship," the man said. "Think if me as a relative, if that helps."

Mae arched a brow. "I know my mother's relatives, and you're not among them. I ask you again to leave before anyone sees you."

"You...you really wish me to go?" The man looked as if his world had shattered around him.

Not just looked, but felt. She could *feel* his anguish as if it were her own. For a moment she hesitated, not wanting to put either of them through the torment.

Then she remembered her father's rage, pushed through her own feelings (his feelings? Their feelings?) and said, "Yes."

He started to turn, then said, "One last thing. A gift for you."

She knew she shouldn't accept gifts from strange men, especially ones who somehow magically appeared in her private rooms.

But she was intrigued, too.

"All right," she said.

He held up his hand, fingers close together and pointed upwards. A small flame appeared, dancing over his fingertips. He sketched a small bow and extended his arm towards her.

As if in a dream, she slowly reached out and let him place the flame in her palm.

The flame shifted, taking the form of a small bird, which

opened its beak and trilled a series of sweet notes. The sound was accompanied by tiny sparks, as if the music had form, drifting into the air.

The bright tune was one Mae's mother used to sing to her, with words she hadn't understood. One she'd forgotten until this moment, and her heart clenched.

Then the bird collapsed into a shower of sparks and was gone.

"If you ever wish to see me, simply speak my name: Ald."

Mae looked up to ask the man what had just happened, but he had already turned away, and was melting again into flame and joining with the fire on the hearth.

Mae staggered backwards until the backs of her knees hit her settee, and then she collapsed onto it. Her mind and emotions spun like the wheels of a train, with all the accompanying noise, it seemed, thundering in her head.

What had just happened? And how, and who was the strange, magical man?

～

As much as she tried, Mae couldn't forget the strange man who placed fire in her hand as if it were no more than a piece of paper folded to look like a bird.

If she were truthful with herself, she'd have to face the feeling that she thought of him often because she missed him that his absence made her feel less whole somehow.

But she shoved those feelings and thoughts aside, because to see Ald was to betray her father.

So she focused her attention on playing with fire.

She had no fear of it—she never had, really. She'd smothered the embers on Nanny's dress without hesitation, with no thought that she might suffer burns.

Embracing the Flames

The man's brief gift convinced her to see what she could actually do, if anything.

Hovering her palm close over a lit candle gave her no injury, nor did sticking her hand boldly into the fireplace flames. The sensation was warm, oddly comforting, not hot or painful.

Next she held her hand close to the fire, close enough that her fingers caressed the flames, and when she drew her hand back, a tiny fire flickered on her fingertip until she blew it out. The ability caused a thrill to course through her, a delighted shiver.

Soon she could light a candle or gas lamp by simply pointing at it and willing it to catch, and could snuff it out by pinching her fingers

She could create simple shapes from the flames, but not anything close to what Ald had done with creating the singing bird.

She wanted to, though. She wanted more, even as she knew to hide her ability from everyone.

She did glean some information from her mother's book, which somehow she now knew was called a grimoire. Since meeting Ald, she had been able to read small portions of it.

Mae's mother had told her stories of witches' familiars, but from the book she learned that they were not pets or servants, but rather were equal companions who assisted witches by enhancing their magic. She couldn't understand all the words, but that seemed to be the gist of it.

Mae lay awake, staring at the tapestry canopy above her bed. In the darkness, she couldn't see the color or pattern, just a hint of heavy fabric.

The more she was able to glean from the grimoire, the more she wanted, but she was stuck.

It was as if Ald had unlocked the beginnings of the ability for her, but only the beginnings.

But Ald was the enemy. Her mother's relationship with him had nearly destroyed her beloved father.

Then again, if time spent with him meant Mae would have greater understanding of what she was able to do, and what she could read, and the answer to all the oh so many questions whirling in her brain, keeping her awake, causing her to make mistakes on her tutor's lessons, well...perhaps she would have to take the chance.

Even if it felt like a betrayal.

∼

THE NEXT DAY, Mae stoked the fire in her sitting room, wrung her hands, and finally said, "Ald, I would like you to return, if you will. I have questions."

The fire shivered at her words. Then, slowly, a shape coalesced into that of a man.

Ald.

Mae felt a rush of warmth, not from the fire, but from his presence. As if she could breathe more deeply now that he was here.

She didn't understand it, but now, with him standing before her again, she was forced to admit how his presence made her feel. Safe. Whole. Fully *herself*.

It was one of the many questions she needed to ask him. Now that he was here, though, she forgot everything she'd listed in her head to say.

The relief on Ald's face mirrored her own.

"I'm glad you reached out to me," he said. "How are you?"

"Confused. Curious." She waved a hand. "So many things."

"Are you concerned about having a strange man in your rooms?" he asked.

"Yes. No... All right, yes, but my father is at his business office and the servants are busy elsewhere."

"Very well," he said. He was formal, holding himself straight, proper. When she gestured to the settee, he sat as far away from her as possible, as if afraid that he would offend her and she would send him away again.

How did she know that?

"What do you wish to know?" he asked.

"Ald. It's a strange name." A stupid question, but the first one that tripped from her lips.

"You wouldn't be able to pronounce my true name, so this is what your mother gave me. Simple, so that in a time of crisis, you can call me easily. Additionally, names have power, and creatures such as us are deeply private."

"Creatures such as you."

"I am what you would call one of the fae folk, or a faerie," he said. "A spirit of nature, of earth and sky and all else. More specifically, I was your mother's familiar, and if you would have me, I would bond with you to be yours as well."

"The book—the grimoire—said that familiars enhance a witch's powers, but I don't understand what that means," Mae said.

"We cannot do magic," Ald said, "but we *are* magic. A witch does magic, channeling their familiar's energy for their spells."

"So, my mother was a witch?" It seemed like a fanciful, ridiculous notion, but Mae already half-believed it must be true.

"Yes, a hedgewitch, one who works with nature or the natural world. Your mother's affinity was for fire, as is yours."

Mae choked out a laugh. "I'm not a witch."

Another fanciful notion...but she *could* play with fire....

Ald smiled for the first time, cocked an already arched brow. "Are you sure of that?"

"No," Mae admitted. "Perhaps I am, or could be, but I understand almost nothing."

"That's part of why I'm here," Ald said. "To help you learn about your mother's powers, and yours, and the grimoire." He took a deep breath. "That is, if you'll have me."

The agreement was on the tip of Mae's tongue, ready to tumble from her lips. A simple yes. Her entire being yearned for it. She could almost feel the closeness, the way they would have a symbiotic relationship, two halves of a whole.

But her voice wouldn't work. The word stuck, tangled in another emotion, more powerful and painful and wormed into the core of her.

Guilt.

When Ald touched her lightly on the hand and asked what was wrong, she realized she was crying. Tears slipping down her cheeks unbidden, their saltiness coating her lips.

"It's all my fault," she whispered, unable to choke the words out louder. "I shouldn't have told Papa about you. It hurt him so, so very badly. And everything of my mother's—except for the grimoire, which I stole—he sent away. He wanted no part of her to remain in the house, because the memory would be too painful for him."

Now Ald's hand settled over hers, a faraway comfort that didn't quite touch her pain.

"You were young," he said. "You didn't understand what you'd seen between your mother and I, and you didn't understand how it would appear to your father. Your question to him was out of innocence, not malice. You are blameless."

"But I'm not," she insisted. "That's not all of it. He rid himself, this house, and *me* of everything of hers. Other than the grimoire, I have nothing. It's as if I caused my mother to be sent away. I destroyed her memory."

"No," Ald said softly, and now his words seemed to penetrate her grief. "Her memory lives on, through me but also through you. You are her daughter, and as a witch, her heir. Your mother is mother is always with you—all you have to do is look into the flames and feel your mother's love warming your heart."

Though she couldn't quite accept it yet, Mae could feel the weight of the words, the truth of them.

"Then yes," she said, her tears now of hope. "I accept you as my familiar. I want to learn to be as good a woman—a witch—as my mother was."

It—and Ald—were her connection to her mother.

This was her legacy.

She would love her father always, and she would also do her mother proud.

ABOUT THE AUTHOR

Dayle A. Dermatis is the author or coauthor of many novels (including snarky urban fantasies Ghosted, Shaded, and Spectered) and more than a hundred short stories in multiple genres, appearing in such venues as Fiction River, Alfred Hitchcock's Mystery Magazine, and DAW Books.

Called the mastermind behind the Uncollected Anthology project, she also guest edits anthologies for Fiction River, and her own short fiction has been lauded in many year's best anthologies in erotica, mystery, and horror.

She lives in a book- and cat-filled historic English-style cottage in the wild greenscapes of the Pacific Northwest. In her spare time she follows Styx around the country and travels the world, which inspires her writing.

Find out more about Dayle at:
dayledermatis.com

facebook.com/dayledermatis
twitter.com/dayledermatis
bookbub.com/authors/dayle-a-dermatis

THE FEMALE TRIUMVIRATE

REBECCA M. SENESE

Even with the thick, fabric pulled back from the windows, the breeze that blew in from the city street was hot and humid. Julia leaned back against the pillows of the lounge chair. Even with this many pillows, the chair felt lumpy and uncomfortable. She shifted, trying for comfort but it seemed impossible. Even the thin white dress she wore felt tight but of course it was, stretching over her swollen belly.

Julia smiled, resting a hand on the growing expanse.

If she had not been waiting for Grandmother she would already have retired to a room deeper in the house, one where the stone walls stayed cool in the heat of the Roman day.

Julia sighed, tasting the dust drifting in from the window. Murmuring voices drifted in, friends hailing each other, merchants hawking their wares, masters instructing their slaves, all mingled into the background.

The baby in her belly kicked. Julia rubbed her belly and shifted again. Such a strong kick. Certainly it must be a boy. A warrior like her husband Pompey the Great or her father Gaius Julius Caesar.

It was too hot to be sitting in this room at this hour. Julia felt sweat dampen her dress. Her hair, curled and styled, stuck to her cheeks. The stone walls seemed to bleed off the heat quicker in the smaller rooms but she was supposed to wait here, in the main room by the window. That was what the dream had told her. Besides, she kept a bowl of water by her lounge chair. She dipped her fingers in and trailed them down her neck. It helped to cool her in the hot Rome afternoons.

She kept a bowl beside her bed at night as well. Then sometimes when Pompey lay with her, she would drip some water onto his chest, watching the droplets mat the greying hairs as they ran along his skin.

She never had long to watch before he would take her in his arms.

Julia gave a sigh. She knew how the people talked, how they sneered. Pompey the Great loved his wife. Such a scandal, such a womanly thing to do when he should be out cavorting with other women. Instead he preferred to be with his wife. Like she had cast a spell on him.

Little did they know, that was not the spell she was being called to cast.

Let them sneer, miserable senators. They did not sneer to her face. She was a woman and not that important. But she was also the daughter of Gaius Julius Caesar. She had only to let her father know how people laughed...

And they would laugh no more.

A slave entered and bowed low.

"The lady Aurelia is here."

"Show her in," Julia said. "Has the other arrived yet?"

The slave shook his head and retreated, hurrying away. Julia spread the white fabric of her dress across her belly and sighed. It was bad enough to request the presence of such a foreigner in her house but to have to wait as well...

"Julia."

Aurelia, her Grandmother, stood in the doorway. Even at sixty-seven, she was every inch the perfect Roman matron, standing proud and erect, a look of no nonsense on her wide face.

Julia pushed up from the lounge chair. She stifled the groan that wanted to come out from her lips as she stood up. She balanced with one hand on the chair.

"I am honoured, Mother," she said.

A smile broke the stern look on her Grandmother's face. Wrinkles creased around her eyes and mouth, reminding Julia of laughing tales at Aurelia's knee. Then Aurelia stepped forward to embrace her.

"All hail well to you, child," Aurelia said. "Lay now. I see how wince. Remove those sandals. Your feet will feel better."

Julia sank down on the lounge chair. Instantly Aurelia dropped to her knees and began removing Julia's sandals.

"Grandmother," Julia cried out.

"Hush and let me finish."

Her fingers felt cool against Julia's hot flesh. Within moments, she had untied the sandals and pulled them off Julia's feet. Relief was instant. Julia leaned back.

This was better than waking from the horrid dream. The one that had called Aurelia here. And that foreigner, whenever she would arrive.

Aurelia rubbed her feet. "Better, yes?"

Julia smiled at her Grandmother. "Yes."

Aurelia finished and tucked her feet under the folds of her dress.

Just then the baby in Julia's belly kicked hard. Julia groaned.

"A kicker," Aurelia said. She rubbed a hand over Julia's belly, pressing just a little. The kicking subsided.

"He must be a boy," Julia said. "He has the fight of a warrior in him."

"You think a girl does not have the fight of a warrior?" Aurelia asked. "It is us who raise those warriors."

"Yes, Mother," Julia agreed in a formal tone. She bowed her head to show the proper respect but her Grandmother did not reply as the slave returned.

"The Greekess has arrived," he said.

"Show her in," Aurelia said, as usual taking on the role of hostess. It never mattered what house she was in, Aurelia's strong personality overpowered all others. Julia had seen it time and again and tried to emulate it. She managed most of the time, but only when Aurelia was not there. When she was, Julia bowed to her will like she had while growing up under her Grandmother's tutelage.

The slap of sandals on marble shook her out of her reverie. Julia pushed up onto an elbow and looked back over her shoulder. For another Roman, she would have risen from her lounge, but this was a foreigner, and a mere child at that. Even if this child was the joint regent of Egypt.

The girl had dark brown skin and hair so black it shimmered in the afternoon light. She wore a plain white Roman dress but gold bands around her wrist and waist marked her as distinctly foreign. Yet instead of being furtive, she stood tall and proud, as if she was the mistress of this house and expected Julia and her Grandmother to submit.

"You are late," Aurelia said.

"I arrive at the time I am set to arrive," the girl said. "I am the one with the longest journey, yet there is no wine and food offered to me. Shall I return home?"

Aurelia pressed her lips together. She was getting ready for a sharp retort, one that could endanger this meeting. Julia knew the signs. She pushed herself up to a sitting position.

"I am Julia and this is my grandmother, Aurelia," she said. "I welcome you to my home and bid you enter. Wine and food will be brought at the end of our meeting, as ordained by the gods. I am the one who entreated you here, by the dreams sent from the gods. Did you not dream them also?"

The girl's tense, defiant expression relaxed. She nodded. "I did dream it. It is why I travelled so far, to help prevent such bloodshed." She bowed her head to Julia. "I am Cleopatra, daughter of Ptolemy XII Auletes, king of Egypt."

From the corner of her eye, Julia saw the tightening of her Grandmother's forehead. Before she could speak, Julia waved the girl toward another lounge chair.

"As ordained, let us discuss," she said.

The girl moved across the room, head held high, hips swaying from side to side under the flowing dress. When she sat, she did not lean back like a civilized person but sat upright, her hands on her knees.

Julia suppressed a sigh. There was only so much one could ask of a foreigner. She supposed it was enough that the girl had come properly dressed.

"Shall I begin?" the girl Cleopatra asked.

Julia nodded. Aurelia stood straight at the head of her lounge chair as if to protect her. After a moment, she bowed her head as well.

"I dreamed of battles," the girl said. "Great slaughter in hot sands. The death of an old Roman senator. Then armies marching out of Rome, to fight other Romans. Then the man with the laurel crown who comes to me in Egypt to be my husband in all but name. I beg him to stay with me but he returns to Rome to be murdered by his colleagues."

Julia shuddered at the description. Except for some details, it was the same dream as hers.

"And what of us?" Aurelia asked. "Did you not dream of us?" She held out her hand to encompass both herself and Julia.

For the first time, the girl dropped her gaze, looking away from them.

"Speak up," Aurelia commanded.

The girl, joint regent of Egypt, started at the sharpness in Aurelia's voice and, like any other person, could not disobey. No one could disobey Julia's Grandmother when she used *that* tone, not even her father who was now a great general.

The girl swallowed. "You are both dead."

Julia blinked at the sting of tears in her eyes. It was the exact same dream. First Aurelia would die then Julia, as she gave birth to her child. She rubbed a hand across her belly, feeling the child stir within her. According to her dream, her child would not live a week, leaving her dearest Pompey devastated and alone. For such a strong man, he was too weak emotionally to survive long without a loving wife. He would marry again, she knew, but her death would destroy his bonds with her father, and with that, set them against each other and destroy them both.

She shuddered at the dream memory of his headless corpse and her father falling under the knives. Both great men, both murdered. Too much bloodshed after too many decades of bloodshed.

Leading Rome down an even bloodier path.

There had to be another way.

"This is why we are here," she said. "To stop this dream from becoming real. The gods have given us this warning. It is up to us to heed it and lead the way."

"How can this be stopped?" Cleopatra asked.

Julia caught the same questioning look from her Grandmother. Julia had been the one to call them here but she had not told them what she proposed.

Now or never.

"We shall do like the ancients," Julia said. "We shall call to the gods, call down great magic to cast a spell that will prevent such destruction. We will give sacrifice to the gods. A life for our lives."

The girl sprang up from her chair. "You mean to kill me."

She headed for the door.

"No," Julia called to her. "You are important to the future, to stability in Egypt. You are not the sacrifice, you are one of the casters."

The girl stopped before she reached the door. She retraced her steps, her sandals shhing across the floor as she moved.

"This is not Roman treachery?" she asked.

"You question my granddaughter's honour?" Aurelia snapped. She pushed herself up to a standing position. Only the slight tremble in her legs told Julia how much of an effort it was.

Before Cleopatra could respond, Julia held up her hands.

"We are not here to argue. The ritual calls for three. The three who have dreamed the dream and that is each of us. We are all honour bound to see it through." She tilted her head toward the girl. "You did not mention your end. I saw you trapped in your own tomb, captured by Roman legionaries, a prisoner instead of an ally, and to avoid being paraded in chains through the streets of Rome, you kill yourself with the bite of a snake. It is many years from now but not that many. Do you not wish to avoid that fate?"

The girl held herself upright, rigid and expressionless, but the paleness that crept over her dark face betrayed her fear.

"I would avoid it," she said.

Julia nodded. "Then we are agreed. We will perform the spell tonight and change our fates as per the message from the gods."

"Agreed," Aurelia said.

Cleopatra nodded. "Agreed. But who will be this sacrifice you speak of?"

Julia rubbed her belly.

"My child. I will give him to the gods and our magic will arise."

※

THEY ADJOURNED to the chamber Julia had prepared over the last few weeks. It had taken her all that time to gather everything together, to prepare the small, round room. The walls washed until they gleamed and the painted with the darkest red she could find. The beautiful robes of silk, the polished copper bowls, the baskets of fruit, ripe and fresh, melons, and olives, and figs overflowing. All of it gathered on the low stone table that sat in the middle of the room. On the floor, she had painted a circle in black all around the table. Julia had done it herself, kneeling on the hard tiles, her back aching as she spread the ink. It would have been easier to command a slave to do it but she couldn't. It had to be completed by her. It was part of the ritual.

"Let us begin," she said.

Aurelia stepped forward, picking up two of the robes. After a moment's hesitation, she held out one to Cleopatra. With head high, the girl stepped forward to accept it. As Aurelia passed the robe to her, Julia noticed the small of movements of the older woman's head, the slightest of bows. For all her regal bearing, Cleopatra responded with her own slight movement.

Julia breathed out, releasing the last tension that clenched at the base of her skull.

Maybe this would work after all. If the three of them, different generations, different traditions, even different lands, could come together, perhaps their ritual could save the republic after all.

Or if not save it, then save the men they all loved or in Cleopatra's case, would love.

"Julia, are you awake, child?"

Aurelia's teasing voice caught her attention. Julia's cheeks warmed. She took the robe Aurelia held out to her.

"Just reflecting on what we are to do," she said.

"Enough reflecting," Cleopatra said. "We must now do."

Julia nodded. "Yes, we must now do."

She slipped the silk robe over her shoulders. The fabric felt cool and smooth on her bare arms. The hood of the robe covered her head, tickling her forehead as it draped down in front of her eyes. It obscured the entire room, leaving only the view of the low table in the centre of the circle. The copper bowls gleamed in the candle light. The fruits looked lush and full, swelling the way her belly swelled.

Julia stepped back until she stood just inside the circle. Lifting her head, she could see Aurelia and Cleopatra doing the same at equal distance around the circle. Julia bowed her head and took a breath.

This was the most difficult part. Giving in to the magic without knowing or understanding. Just trusting.

She had to trust. She had to believe. It was the only way to save her precious Pompey. The only way to save her father, save the Republic.

Save herself.

She lifted her arms and began to chant.

The other women's voices joined hers. She heard them, felt them mingling in the air. Rising as she lifted her arms higher, wider, to engulf the circle. The air began to feel warm, to crackle with energy the way it did before a thunderstorm.

The gods. It was the power of the gods, coming to them, hearing their call, bringing forth their magic.

Her voice trembled. She took a deep breath and her voice steadied.

They called to the gods, calling, inviting, entreating, proclaiming. They offered the fruit of the table, the precious bowls and rare jewels, the delicious spices.

Julia offered the child in her womb.

The air pressed against her, smelling thick with soot. She coughed and continued chanting. Energy prickled on her skin, making the robe stick to her arms. She rolled her shoulders but the fabric continued to bind against her. Like it was some kind of funeral shroud.

She was too young for a funeral shroud.

Still the fabric constricted, squeezing tighter and tighter around her. It pressed the air from her lungs then stopped her from taking a deep breath. She felt it pulling on her arms, trying to pull them down to her sides. She fought against it, strained to keep her arms outstretched, to call to the gods.

The air crackled around her, the way it did when a storm was brewing. The candles flickered as if a wind blew but that was impossible. This room had no window, just the stones walls painted red, as if dripped with blood. A reminder that blood magic was the strongest magic of all.

Julia's heart pounded. She tried to suck in air. It tasted of smoke and cloves and spices that burned her nostrils. It felt so hot now. She was tired, so tired. All she wanted to do was lie down, to rest. Her back ached. Her belly ached. The child within kicked and kicked again.

And the robe...

The robe tightened around her, making it hard to breathe, hard to chant.

But she would not stop. Even as her breath became shallow and her head felt lighter.

She felt her body sway.

What was it she asked? What did she wish to treat from the gods?

Please, save her husband, save her father, save the Republic. Save them all...

The air thickened around her, the scent of burning spices choked her, dark smoke blotted out the walls.

She felt tingling at her temples...

The next thing she was aware of was Aurelia's face hovering above her. Behind her Grandmother's head, she saw the girl Cleopatra bending over her, concern etched onto her narrow features.

"What happened?" Julia asked. Her voice came out like a croak. She took a breath. The air seemed sweeter, clearer.

"You fell over," Cleopatra said.

"You fainted," Aurelia said. "Come, sit up child."

The old woman slipped an arm around her shoulders and helped Julia to sit up on the floor. The low table was on her left. Candles flickered on the corners. Thin trails of smoke rose from the flames but the dark billowing smoke that blotted out the walls had vanished. She noticed the bowls were empty.

All the food was gone.

"Did it work?" she asked. "Are the gods satisfied with our sacrifice?"

Aurelia exchanged a quick glance with Cleopatra.

"When you fell, the candles snuffed out," she said. "A blast of cold filled the room and then great warmth. A moment later the candles were burning again and the food was gone. You lay on the floor. Only then did we break the circle to come to you."

"It worked," Cleopatra said. "The old woman does not wish to say it but it did. I can feel it."

Aurelia's expression hardened but she did not contradict the girl. Instead she put Julia's arm over her shoulder.

"Stand now, child."

Cleopatra moved to Julia's other side and together they helped her stand. As Julia felt her legs under her, the robe loosened and fell away, revealing the stain of blood on her dress.

The gods had taken her sacrifice after all.

~

POMPEY WAS DISTRAUGHT when he returned home to find she had miscarried. She blamed it on the upheaval in the city, roving gangs of thugs that disrupted the peace.

She asked him to write to her father about it.

The correspondence focused Pompey's support on her father and away from the Senate. Soon the two of them decided on a strategy to restore peace in the city. A body of soldiers responsible to the consul would patrol and enforce the laws of the city.

Then months later, when her father finished his pacification of Gaul and was returning home, Julia found herself pregnant again. She retreated to the inner room. It had been sealed since the day the three of them had cast their spell, entreated the gods, whatever you could call the bargain they had made.

The black circle still ringed the floor, just slightly smudged where she had fallen. Candles, having burned and stuck to the floor, ringed the low table. The table was bare except for three copper bowls. Julia filled them with the fruit she had brought with her. She had been saving it for an offering to the Good Goddess, but it seemed more appropriate now.

She needed to know if she would have to sacrifice again.

By the time she finished lighting the candles, the air seemed to smell of the strange, exotic perfume Cleopatra had worn. At the same time, Julia could almost feel the solid, stoic presence of Aurelia behind her. She had not seen her Grandmother since the sacrifice, but it felt like she was here in the room.

Like both of them were here in the room with her.

With a grunt, Julia lowered herself to the floor and sat just inside the black circle near the spot with the smudge. Her original spot the day of the sacrifice. It seemed like the right place.

Placing her hands on her knees, she closed her eyes and breathed in. The scent of Cleopatra's perfume, musky with spice, tickled her nostrils. The warmth of Aurelia's arm felt like a secure support around Julia's shoulders.

They were here. She could feel them.

It gave her courage. Reminded her of who she was. A strong Roman woman. She would do what needed to be done to secure her family and by doing so, the future of Rome.

"Oh Good Goddess, I call upon you," she said. "Do you demand another sacrifice to keep Rome safe?"

She fell silent and waited. In the stillness, she felt the air thicken and press against her. Was the Good Goddess testing her resilience? She had already made the most terrible of sacrifices. But if she had to she would do it again.

The grip of her hands on her knees pinched her nails into her skin. Still she felt nothing but the thickness in the air. No smoke thickened in the room. No burning spices choked her. No message from the Good Goddess, nothing from any of the gods.

Were they not listening because she was alone?

But the others were here. She could feel their presence. Cleopatra and Aurelia. The three of them in this room had conjured the gods and left an indelible imprint here. That imprint supported her now. It was enough. It had to be enough.

Then the pressure, the heat, seemed to dissipate. The room felt empty. Cooler.

Julia opened her eyes.

The fruit was gone. The empty copper bowls glinted in the flickering candlelight.

Julia touched her dress. She did not feel faint and there was no stain of blood.

The gods had taken the fruit as payment and been satisfied.

Relief made her sag and it took a moment before she pushed herself up off the floor. As she steadied herself she touched her belly. Her child still lived.

Blessed by the gods.

By the time that her father was crossing back into Italy, Julia's belly swelled with child. Although Pompey had relinquished his role as consul, he still directed the soldiers patrolling the streets and keeping the peace. When calls came to grant her father a triumph for all his work in Gaul, Pompey was leading the calls.

Julia wanted to attend but her pregnancy was too far along. From her bedroom window, she could hear the cheers reverberating through the streets. Aurelia held her hand as the pain pierced Julia, filling her with the desperate need to push. Her own screams were drowned out by the yelling from outside.

By the time Pompey returned from the celebrations, Julia was able to present him with a son.

Her husband, who had once been known as the teenage butcher, wept at the sight of their son and insisted his name be Julius Lucius Scarbonius Pompey.

A short time later, her father arrived, trailing Aurelia. From the smile on Aurelia's face, Julia knew her Grandmother had called for Gaius Julius Caesar.

Julia had not seen him for many years and could see how the war in Gaul had shaped him. The sharpness along his jaw. The definition of his muscles through his toga, almost gaunt. Only the smile on his face and the tears shimmering in his eyes reflected his more gentle side. He knelt by her bed to embrace her.

Then Pompey brought forth their son to present to his grandfather.

At Pompey's recitation of the child's name, Julia saw a look pass between her father and her husband.

They had been bound together by desire for power and control and by her marriage to Pompey. Now they were family, bound by the child in her husband's arms. Nothing would ever break them apart.

The child began to fuss. His cries made Julia's heart ache.

"Bring him to me," she said and held her arms out to her husband.

He deposited the boy into her arms then turned to her father.

"We have much to discuss," he said.

"Let us dine and do so," her father said.

Together, the men left the room.

As they disappeared down the hall, Aurelia turned to Julia. "Now it begins," she said.

∼

THE NEXT YEAR, Pompey was confirmed as governor of Hispania for a further five years along with Julius Caesar as governor in Gaul for the same length of time. But just before Caesar was to leave again for Gaul, a revolt in Egypt demanded attention. Caesar struck out to deal with it.

There he met the young Cleopatra.

Although Rome would never accept this foreign queen, Caesar eventually divorced his wife and married Cleopatra. Soon Julia learned they had children, the eldest one a daughter named Cerina.

By this time, Pompey and Caesar continued to rule jointly, trading consulships with governorships and back again. The solders patrolling the streets in Rome kept the peace but also cowed the Senate into agreeing with the rule as much as they wailed about the Republic. But even as they wailed, they could not help acknowledge how much better things were. New buildings of marble and stone replaced crumbling brick. Well-made roads brought a flood of riches to the city. Farms prospered in the country.

And a dynasty was being forged.

Julius Lucius was only ten when Aurelia finally died peacefully in her sleep but he still wept in Julia's arms. As the days passed, he withdrew from his studies, preferring to sit quietly with his scrolls. Julia tried to distract him, telling him about the latest set of games but the boy refused to attend.

Julia withdrew and for the first time in many years, made her way to the small room in the centre of the house.

She had forbade anyone from entering this room so when

she finally opened the door, she expected to be greeted by dust. But the stone floor was smooth and polished. The colour on the walls still vivid as if only completed the day before. The copper bowls gleamed as she lit the candles, brightening the area. Even the air smelled fresh and clean, not musty or humid.

The gods favoured this room. A room of power and magic.

Julia filled the bowls with the fruit she had brought. Luscious melons, ripe grapes, sweet berries, fresh olives and figs that filled the air with a delicious aroma.

Julia kept her head bowed as she stepped back from the bowls and knelt at the edge of the black circle. The mark still looked as fresh as the first time she had drawn it so many years ago. Further testament to the will of the gods.

Closing her eyes, she breathed in the heady scent of the candles mingling with the ripe fruit. She felt her muscles loosen. Her mouth drew slack then seemed to move of its own accord. She mumbled words she did not know but she suspected their purpose.

Calling for the blessings of the gods.

Calling to Cleopatra.

Then between one breath and the next, the air changed. Gone was the ripeness of the fruit and the sharp sting of the candles. Instead she breathed in a rich, spicy musk.

Julia opened her eyes.

She was kneeling in a room draped with rich, colourful fabrics. Golds and reds and vibrant blues. Instead of the stone floor under her knees, she knelt on a thick, woven rug. To her right was a low table covered with copper bowls filled with spiced meats. But the person in front of her caught her attention.

Even before the woman lifted her head, Julia recognized Cleopatra.

The girl Julia had known had ripened into a woman with a

thin, narrow face. Robes of white and gold swirled around her kneeling form, accentuating the lines of her body. She took a deep breath and opened her eyes. A slight smile creased her lips then faded.

"I am sorry about Aurelia," she said.

Pain pierced Julia but she pushed it away. There was time to grieve later. Now was the time reaffirm their bond.

And their goals.

"She performed all her duties as a great Roman woman," Julia said. "I strive to follow her example. Now we must honour her life by moving forward."

Cleopatra bowed her head.

"Agreed. But we must replace Aurelia as soon as possible to continue our pact. The two must become three again for the glory of Egypt and of Rome."

"You have someone in mind," Julia said.

"I do," Cleopatra said. "I propose Cerina."

"She is a child," Julia said.

"True but she is not much younger than I was when you brought me into your triumvirate. She will learn from us and carry our mission into the future."

Julia hesitated. When she had agreed to Aurelia's scheme of building a triumvirate and enlisting the gods on their behalf, it had been to stabilize the teetering Republic of Rome, to save it from the violence and destruction that threatened it. Now it was at peace and prospered.

What would continuing the triumvirate lead to?

Julia closed her eyes and breathed deeply. After a moment, the vision of the gods flooded into her, flashing image after image into her mind, too fast for her to comprehend most of them. But a few she could grasp at.

The influence of Rome, partnered with Egypt, spreading across the continent, overwhelming and incorporating all before it, including a minor, monotheistic cult of Jews. It became supplanted by the empire of Rome as it absorbed all, bringing peace and stability. Spreading even across a distance ocean on the other side of Gaul, joining with tall, dark-haired natives who had their own versions of the gods.

All living to their own customs under the might of a Roman imperator.

Chosen, influenced, and guided by the female triumvirate on behalf of the gods.

Julia opened her eyes to find Cleopatra studying her. Lines of tension deepened around her mouth but she did not speak.

It was up to Julia to decide.

Julia straightened her shoulders. Past Cleopatra, pressed against the doorway, Julia spotted the girl child Cerina. Thin-faced like her mother but a strong chin and nose like her father.

Julia's own father.

Julia waved the child into the room.

"Step forward," she said. "Join our triumvirate and let us take Rome, and Egypt, into the future."

The child hesitated and for a moment, Julia thought she might decline. That although born of the bold Egyptian queen and Julia's own conqueror father, Cerina might have none of that strong courage in her heart.

Then the child straightened her shoulders in a movement that quite matched Julia's own and stepped into the room toward the two kneeling women.

"I am ready," the girl child said. Her voice rang strong and true.

Ready to embrace the future and fulfill the will of the gods.

Jupiter be praised.

ABOUT THE AUTHOR

Based in Toronto, Canada, I write horror, science fiction and mystery/crime, often all at once in the same story. I am the author of the contemporary fantasy series, the *Noel Kringle Chronicles* featuring the son of Santa Claus working as a private detective in Toronto. Garnering an Honorable Mention in "*The Year's Best Science Fiction*" and nominated for numerous Aurora Awards, my work has appeared in *Pulphouse Fiction Magazine, Bitter Mountain Moonlight: A Cave Creek Anthology, Promise in the Gold: A Cave Creek Anthology, Home for the Howlidays, Unmasked: Tales of Risk and Revelation, Obsessions: An Anthology of Original Stories, Fiction River: Visions of the Apocalypse, Fiction River: Sparks, Fiction River: Recycled Pulp, Tesseracts 16: Parnassus Unbound, Ride the Moon, Imaginarium 2012, Tesseracts 15: A Case of Quite Curious Tales, TransVersions, Deadbolt Magazine, On Spec, The Vampire's Crypt, Storyteller, Reflection's Edge, Future Syndicate* and *Into the Darkness*, amongst others.

Find me online:
www.RebeccaSenese.com

- facebook.com/Rebecca.M.Senese
- twitter.com/RebeccaSenese
- bookbub.com/authors/rebecca-m-senese
- amazon.com/~/e/B004LYV91A

IN THE BANYAN COPSE

DEBBIE MUMFORD

CHAPTER ONE

Kanti Misra leaned from the window of her sleeping bower and breathed in the sweet scents of leaf and bark, orchids and sunlit sky. Lovingly, she caressed a broad, shiny leaf of her family's banyan tree. "Thank you for another night's shelter," she murmured and felt the leaf shiver in response. The tree's contentment wafted through her consciousness, bestowing calmness of spirit in its wake. Kanti smiled, and trailing her hand across the living walls of her bower, began her preparations for the day.

She would be training one of the younger banyans in the copse today, so she chose working garments, an unadorned green sari wrapped to create pants paired with the cropped top of an unbleached muslin choli. With deft fingers, she combed and braided her long dark hair.

Bestowing a final pat on the wall of her bower, she stepped onto a broad limb, ran lightly across to the trunk and padded down a section of the staircase that wove around and through the huge tree's trunk and many large aerial roots. Navigating the many twists and turns with long familiarity, she emerged into the ground floor kitchen where her mother and several other copse women were already at work preparing the morning meal.

Though on the ground in the shade of the wide canopy of the huge banyan, the communal kitchen was light and airy. A cool breeze wafted through the open-weave of the walls, mitigating the heat from the ovens and stirring the enticing fragrances of fresh cut fruit, dried spices and flatbread still warm from the oven

"Good morning, Amma," Kanti said, bending to kiss her mother's cheek as the older woman prepared colorful dishes of fruit chutney to go with the morning's flatbread.

"Good morning to you, my sweetling," her mother, Devi Misra, replied without looking up.

Kanti moved across the room, picked up a silver knife and began cutting flatbread into quarters. She'd accumulated a good-sized pile when her mother shrieked.

"Kanti! What are you wearing?"

She glanced down to see what was wrong, but all was well. Her choli was in place, modestly covering breasts and shoulders, and her sari was securely wrapped and tied into pants.

Puzzled she answered, "My work clothes, Amma. I'm training banyans today." Then she noticed that her mother wore her best, most lavishly embroidered sari, her dark blue choli decorated with small crystals, like sprays of dewdrops adorning her neck and shoulders.

"For the love of root and branch, daughter," Devi cried striding toward Kanti and shooing her with a brightly colored cloth. "Get back to your bower and adorn yourself properly. The embroidered fuchsia sari, I think, and the petal pink choli. Yes, the one with silver embroidery." She herded Kanti toward the woven stairs, calling instructions with every step. "And rebraid your hair. Plait it with seed pearls. You must look your best today!"

Bewildered, Kanti stumbled past the work tables, but stopped at the entrance to the stairs, clinging to one of the branches forming the doorway to the kitchen.

"But why, Amma? What is happening today?"

Devi Misra drew herself up to her full height, still several inches shorter than her willowy daughter, and announced, "Your betrothed has arrived. Father has gone to lead him to the copse."

Kanti leaned heavily against the door-branch, her legs suddenly as weak as new shoots. Her doom was upon her. He had come.

She glanced up to see the other women watching with interest, and dredging up her last remnants of strength, stood erect, head held high. "Thank you, Amma," she said with dignity. "I'll go to my bower and prepare."

Turning, she left the communal kitchen and began the long climb back to her bower. Her ascent was tediously slow. She'd lost the joy and enthusiasm of the new day. Her feet felt like dead, water-logged wood. Step by weary step she climbed, leaning heavily against the woven hand supports of her beloved banyan.

How could her father have done this to her? How could he have bargained her life away for a trade alliance? To please the Raja of Prandhahar, of course, but the princes of other copses had managed to make advantageous trade alliances without selling their only daughters. Why had her father chosen to ally bloodlines as well as material goods?

She closed her eyes and leaned back against the trunk of her banyan, the bark worn smooth by generations of her kin. The tree's spirit sought her mind, sending tendrils of peace and comfort drifting along her consciousness. She accepted the proffered comfort and small leaf strewn twigs twined around her fingers and wrists.

Melding into her tree, she sought the calm she would need to face the day. The quiet, well-rooted grace that stood tall and strong no matter what storms the elements might throw against it. Gradually, her fear and agitation melted. Thanking the mighty banyan, she stood straight again, caressing the leaves as they released her fingers.

She was a daughter of the banyan as much as she was of the Prince of the Banyan Copse. She would not disgrace her tree or her family. She would bend in this storm, and then stand straight and grow strong.

CHAPTER TWO

Arthur Blakeslee removed his top hat and wiped his sweating brow with the sleeve of his best black damask coat. Was there no shade in this wretched country?

His father's autocarriage had deposited him here nearly an hour before. "Here" being a bare-board platform just outside the border gate barring the road to Prandhahar. A single bench sat in the middle of the small platform, but nothing more. No building. No pavilion. Not even a shade tree growing to the side. And here he had understood that the whole country depended on trees. That Prandhahar had no buildings as he knew them, only living trees trained to grow into shelters for their human masters.

With all the advancements available to civilized men, Arthur couldn't imagine why any sane being would choose to live in a tree. Even if trees existed to be lived in, and he certainly couldn't see any evidence of such a thing. He stood and paced from one end of the small platform to the other, a matter of despairingly few steps.

Where was his guide? His driver had dispatched a

messenger pigeon to Prince Misra before he'd marooned Arthur in this hot, barren place. Surely the bird couldn't have gotten lost or garbled the message. His father had spent a fortune breeding that line of birds from the wild pigeons of Bravenstadt. All the birds in his city-state were sapient and spoke perfectly clearly, but this line, well, their diction and memory were exceptional. No, the prince had surely received the message.

Arthur blew out a breath, replaced his top hat—his head was getting unreasonably warm—and resumed his seat. Undoubtedly, the prince's conveyance was simply slower than that to which Arthur was accustomed. Though he still couldn't imagine any good reason why his father's driver shouldn't have simply taken him all the way to Prince Misra's palace.

Certainly, there was a gate across the road here at the border, but the obstacle was unmanned. The driver could have simply lifted the gate, driven through and then replaced it. Stupid man.

Still, what was it his father had said as Arthur was leaving? Oh yes. "Remember, son, Prandhahar is not Bravenstadt. Be careful not to trample on local customs. I'm sending you to Prandhahar to collect your bride and finalize a profitable alliance, not to instigate a war out of ignorance."

Honestly! As if Arthur were a youngster not yet out of short pants. Why, he'd been negotiating treaties and alliances for the better part of five years. He knew his way around a board room. He'd have this prince eating out of his hand long before the marriage ceremony took place.

Though why his father had felt it necessary to seal this particular alliance with marriage was beyond Arthur. He didn't mind. Not really. As long as the girl wasn't completely abhorrent, he'd manage. But why consummate the agreement with marriage when it was an advantageous trade alliance on both sides already?

Well, no matter. He'd make nice with the Prandhaharans for

a few days then whisk his bride back to Bravenstadt and the civilized industrial society in which he'd grown to manhood. This journey was, after all, only a minor inconvenience in a life of profitable enterprise.

He was just about to remove his hat and wipe his face again when he spied a white clad figure walking toward him from the Prandhaharan side of the border.

Walking? He glanced at his baggage. He had packed lightly, but still, he'd never imagined having to actually carry his own bags. That was what autocarriages were for. He understood that Prandhaharans didn't build mechanical contraptions, but surely they had horses and wagons? Surely a prince wouldn't be walking down the road to collect his future son-in-law? Why, that was unthinkable.

Evidently, what was unthinkable to Arthur was perfectly normal to a Prandhaharan prince, for a few moments later the man stood before him, bowing.

"Arthur Blakeslee?" the man asked.

Arthur nodded. "Have I the pleasure of addressing Prince Sanjit Misra?" He gave the man a small but courteous bow and then eyed his future father-in-law. The man was dark-skinned, with eyes so deep a brown as to be almost black. His hair was completely covered in a white turban, but his brows were midnight black. He wore a long-sleeved white jacket that buttoned all the way to his neck, loose white pants, and simple sandals. He sported no facial hair, nor any adornment upon his person, but his eyes were steady and gleamed with intelligence.

"You have, my son," he said, pressing his hands together before his chest and bowing slightly. "The Banyan Copse is pleased to welcome you to Prandhahar and, in due course, to our family." He glanced at the two large cases resting by the bench. "These are yours?"

Arthur followed his glance and nodded. "Yes. I'm sorry. I wasn't aware we would be walking."

Prince Misra raised an eyebrow and moved to pick up one of the cases. "And how else would one come to our copse?"

Arthur lunged forward and grabbed the larger of the two bags. "Well, in Bravenstadt we travel by autocarriage, though horses and wagons are still employed by the lower classes."

Too late he realized that he might have just implied that the prince was lower class. His face heated, with more than the warmth of the day.

But Prince Misra merely smiled and straightened, adjusting his grip on the case. "We do not believe in mechanical contrivances in Prandhahar," he said mildly. "We prefer to use the bodies the gods have gifted us. Come. Food awaits after an invigorating walk."

Arthur hefted his monogrammed case and followed the prince along the dusty road, wondering what his father had gotten him into now.

CHAPTER THREE

Kanti stood at the window of her bower looking out over the road to Bravenstadt. Soon her father and his guest would appear, and she would meet the man with whom she was to spend her life. The man who would take her away from everything she had ever known, who would carry her away to Bravenstadt to live among heathen miscreants who created mechanical monsters to do their bidding. She would lose her trees and be imprisoned by metal and brick; would lose the wind whispering through leaves, the joyous gurgle of streams, and be surrounded by mechanical whirrs and whistles and who-knew-what other ungodly noise.

Life as she had known it would be over. She would be entombed in an unknown land, imprisoned by a strange man.

She sighed heavily and fought to find again the calm her tree had bestowed earlier. Raising her eyes, she saw her father just coming into view. But something was wrong. The man in white didn't stride purposefully as her father did. This figure faltered, burdened by a figure dressed all in black.

A small shriek escaped her lips and then she was running down the winding stairs, desperate to find her mother.

"Amma!" she called, bursting into Devi Misra's sitting room. "Amma! Father is coming, but something is wrong with his companion. Send someone to help."

Without need for further explanation, Devi leapt to her feet, raced to the window and called down to her kinfolk, "The prince needs assistance. Send men to help him and our guest home."

The patter of feet and the sound of raised voices assured Kanti that her mother's pleas had been heard. Devi turned from the window and resumed her seat, motioning for Kanti to join her.

"Now, tell me what you have seen."

Kanti described her impression, ending with, "Have they sent me a man too infirm to walk, Amma? Surely Father will not wed me to an unfit suitor, even for a profitable trade agreement."

Devi patted her daughter's hand. "Do not borrow trouble, sweetling. We do not know the truth of the matter. Trust your father to make a wise choice."

Kanti lowered her eyes, not wishing to be disrespectful, but not feeling terribly trusting of her father's judgment at that moment.

CHAPTER FOUR

Arthur trudged down the endless road, following his betrothed's father. The man carried the heavy bag as though it weighed nothing, while Arthur's arms screamed in agony at his burden. And the heat, how did these people bear it?

The sun beat down upon the road making the very air dance and shimmer before Arthur's eyes. Sweat dripped down his face, sluiced down his back, and pooled at the base of his spine. His fine clothes were drenched, his feet swimming in their black leather boots. He wanted nothing more than to tear off his clothes and run naked to the nearest stream. Did Prandhahar have streams? It must. Yet he'd seen nothing but the sun-baked road and sere plains stretching to infinity.

He staggered, and the prince dropped the case he carried and steadied him.

"Are you all right, my son?"

Arthur tried to answer, to say that he was fine, but while his skin ran with sweat, his lips and tongue were parched, too dry for words.

Prince Misra pulled Arthur's arm across his shoulder and, leaving the baggage behind, half-carried Arthur forward.

"Do not despair, my son," he said. "You are simply overheated. We are nearly home. Soon you will rest in the shade of the banyan and my daughter will bring you lemonade with honey to drink."

Arthur tried to mumble his thanks, but moving his feet seemed to be all he could manage at the moment. He wondered vaguely about his baggage, about the bride gift he'd brought for the young woman he'd never seen, but worrying required too much effort. He concentrated instead on moving first one foot, then the other.

After what seemed like an eternity, hands lifted him from the prince's shoulders. His weight left his feet and he felt himself borne along the road. Floating. Drifting. The day's brilliance rendering him weightless and free as one of his father's messenger pigeons.

The light faded and he blinked as disembodied hands removed his black damask coat and silk cravat, loosened his collar, and pulled off his boots. Bright colored shapes flitted past his unfocused eyes, like butterflies dancing on a breeze. A cool cloth covered his eyes and consciousness slipped silently away.

"Is he a simpleton, Father? To walk about in the full sun dressed all in black? And those clothes! Who would wear such heavy fabrics in summer?"

Arthur heard the words, noted the melodic voice of the young woman who spoke them, but took a moment to understand that they described him.

When their sense registered, he yanked the cloth from his eyes and sat up. Cool wood met bare feet and Arthur realized the state of his attire. Blood suffused his face while blackness crowded the edges of his vision.

A hand touched his shoulder, restraining him. "Slowly,

young Arthur," Prince Misra said. "You do not wish to lose consciousness again."

Arthur turned his head, perplexed. "Again?"

Prince Misra nodded. "You fainted from the heat on the road. My men carried you home."

Arthur swallowed. His mouth felt thick and cottony and a sour taste lingered on his tongue. He relaxed against the cushions of the divan where he'd been resting. "My apologies, sir. I did not mean to cause you or your people distress."

The prince waved his comments away. "It was nothing. You are unfamiliar with our land and our ways. Rest. My daughter will bring you a cool drink."

For the first time, Arthur noticed the young woman who had been speaking when he regained consciousness. The prince's daughter? Was this beautiful young woman his bride? He lifted a shaky hand to his face and rubbed his eyes. If so, he was an extremely fortunate man.

He tried not to stare, but it was difficult. The bright pink of her garments drew his eye, as did the grace of her movement. Soon she knelt before him, offering him a glass of liquid.

"Thank you," he mumbled, embarrassed to meet his betrothed barefoot and without his coat and cravat.

"Drink," she said. "You are dehydrated. You'll feel better soon."

Arthur obeyed. The liquid soothed his parched mouth, the taste sour and sweet at the same time. He drained the first glass and was handed another, this time by an older woman.

The prince clapped his hands, drawing every eye in the room. "Let us sit," he commanded. "Our introductions have not gone as planned, but that is the way of life. We will become acquainted despite an unusual beginning."

He sat across from Arthur, settling on a low, wide branch of the banyan tree cushioned with a blue and silver pad. The older woman joined him, while the young woman sank onto a low pouf to the side. She was exquisite. Black hair sleekly braided with pearls glinting among the locks, her almond shaped eyes dark and liquid. Light, colorful garments floated around a lithe and willowy body. She was elegant and graceful and completely foreign to his eyes.

"Arthur Blakeslee of Bavenstadt, allow me to present my wife, Princess Devi Misra."

Arthur pulled his attention from the young woman and met the gaze of the prince's wife. Unlike her husband and daughter, Princess Misra's eyes were a clear gray and seemed to see right through him. She smiled, bowing her silk covered head, and murmured, "We are pleased to welcome you to our home, Arthur Blakeslee."

"Thank you, my lady," he replied, lowering his eyes before inclining his head. "Your hospitality is most welcome."

"And this," the prince said, gesturing to the lovely young woman, "is our daughter Kanti, your betrothed wife."

Arthur's breath caught in his throat as he turned his attention once again to the ravishing creature on the pouf. Her head was bowed and she did not meet his gaze. He waited, but when she didn't speak, decided she must be overcome with maidenly shyness.

He cleared his throat and said, "I am honored that you have consented to be my wife, Kanti."

Her head jerked up and she stared at him, eyes blazing. If he'd been standing, he would have taken a step or two back, as it was, he leaned away from her.

"Consented?" she cried, then turned that lethal gaze upon her father. "When did I consent? When was I even consulted regarding this, this...arrangement?"

"Daughter," said the prince, his voice calm but firm, "remember who and where you are. Greet our guest civilly."

Her cheeks flamed, but she lowered her eyes and said, "Welcome, Arthur Blakeslee. I hope you will be at ease in our home."

Arthur sat still, quite plainly astounded. He'd never observed such fire in a young woman. He'd expected a demure maiden, shy and obedient. If this outburst was any indication, he was unlikely to find such a woman in this room.

Collecting himself, he said, "Thank you, Kanti Misra." He'd meant to stop there, but found himself straightening his spine and glaring at her. "And if it makes a difference, no one consulted me either. My father sent me to collect my bride, and here I am. Your obedient servant, madam."

She glanced up, surprise etched on her face. He inclined his head sharply and then turned his attention to her father.

Prince Misra raised a hand to his mouth – hiding a smile perhaps? – cleared his throat and said, "We have much to learn of each other's cultures. That is actually why your father and I decided that a marriage would be more advantageous than a simple signed document.

"You, Arthur, will be an emissary to Prandhahar, helping us understand Bravenstadt. We know that your city-state is very different, but we don't understand why your people choose to live as they do. You will help us see that beyond the obvious differences, our people are much the same."

Arthur nodded. "I understand, sir. It will be my pleasure to provide such a service."

The prince bowed his acknowledgement.

"And you, daughter," he continued. "You will live among the Bravenstadters and will help them understand our beliefs and our ways. You will use your gift among the trees of a far-away land to show your husband's people that not everything need be made of metal and wire."

Kanti's eyes widened, but she kept silent, merely nodding to her father.

"Her gift?" Arthur asked, glancing from father to daughter. "I don't understand, sir."

The prince gestured to their surroundings, and Arthur truly looked at the room for the first time. The walls were smooth, burnished wood, the floor as well, though the wood beneath his bare toes held a different quality to the polished wood floors of his home in Bravenstadt. It was...difficult to put into words, not warm exactly, but somehow *live* as though he could feel the sap pulsing beneath his feet.

Absurd! He was still light-headed from dehydration.

The doorways and windows were bounded by leafy twigs, the view screened not by glass or wire mesh, but by woven saplings with leaves that furled and unfurled according to the room's need for light. The vast beams of the ceiling were branches hung with seed pods and dotted with clinging orchids. The room was cool and secure, but by far the most unusual place he'd ever seen.

He glanced at Prince Misra. "Please explain, sir."

"Kanti is a gifted topiarist," the prince said. "Her spirit joins with the spirits of the trees and through her gift she explains our needs. If it is within the tree's ability to give, they grow at her direction, providing us with shelter and security, but never at the cost of the tree's vitality. Harm the tree; harm the community."

Arthur blinked. "You mean to say that this girl talks to trees...and they obey her?"

The prince nodded. "Crudely put, but accurate."

Arthur jumped to his feet and padded to the window, too agitated to sit still. He gazed out, surprised to find that the room he occupied was some thirty feet above the ground. He stepped back, wondering if the engineering that allowed the height was sound?

Then he laughed at himself. If what he had just heard was

true, there was no engineering. Only the whim of a not yet fully mature girl.

He whirled around and paced back to the divan. "But that's patent nonsense. No one can talk to trees, and even if she could, I'm sure no one in Bravenstadt would be the least bit interested in telling trees to modify their growth habits."

The young woman leapt to her feet and stood facing him, entirely too close for comfort.

"How dare you!" she spat, punctuating each word with a poke of her forefinger against his chest. "How dare you call my father, the Prince of Banyan Copse, a liar? How dare you malign my gift, my power, simply because you're too stupid to understand that there are more things in this world than your mighty Bravenstadt engineers have dreamed of?"

She whirled away from him like some frenzied flower and fell to her knees before her father. "You see, Father? He's ignorant and prejudiced and...and...and narrow-minded! You cannot mean to bind me to such a one for the rest of my life?"

Arthur was incensed. How dare this slip of a...a native girl suggest that he was ignorant?

"Now see here," he cried, "I'm sure my father had no idea that your daughter was so blatantly outspoken and willful. In Bravenstadt a young woman of good breeding would know her place and know when to keep silent while the men arranged matters. This won't do. This won't do at all."

"Silence, both of you," roared the prince coming to his feet and moving away from his imploring daughter. "Kanti, go to your bower. Change into your work clothes and then return to me."

"But..."

He rounded on her with a glare. "Now!"

She rose with a fluid grace that filled Arthur with admiration despite his anger.

"Yes, Father," she whispered and fled the room.

"And you, young man," the prince said, turning to Arthur. "You would do well to keep your opinions to yourself until you have the experience to support them."

"But sir..."

The prince held up a hand to silence him. "Just because you have not experienced a thing does not mean it does not exist. Look around you, man! Prandhahar is not Bravenstadt. Our ways are not your ways, but that does not make either way invalid."

He turned then to his wife, who had waited out the storm of emotions serenely and without comment.

"Devi, please show our guest to his bower and provide him with suitable garments. We don't want him fainting while he's out with Kanti," he said with a smile. "She might leave him to the crows."

Arthur's eyes widened at both the insult to his clothes and to the suggestion that his betrothed might do him bodily harm.

"When you are suitably attired," the prince said to him, "return to this room. You and Kanti must make a start at being emissaries. You can practice on each other."

CHAPTER FIVE

Kanti, dressed once again in the green pants-wrapped sari and plain linen choli, led Arthur Blakeslee through the Banyan Copse, explaining the Prandhaharan way of life as they walked. She glanced sidelong at her companion. Now that he was properly dressed, the man was not unattractive.

Certainly his skin was too pale, but Bravenstadters were known to be light-skinned. She could live with that, would see to it that he left his nasty brick and metal dwelling and learned to spend some time in the wholesome light of the sun. What she found most distressing about his person was the facial hair. Who would want a growth of fur hiding the line of his upper lip? Or the evil little triangle of dark hair obscuring his chin? Was his chin disfigured that he felt the need to hide it?

Her thoughts strayed to the intimacies of marriage and she shuddered. Kiss a man with a furry face? How abhorrent!

She dropped her gaze to the path and continued her discourse on government.

"So, you see, the Raja governs all of Prandhahar from the Arjuna Copse in the center of our land. He is advised by the princes of all the copses, my father being one of his most trusted advisors."

"When you say 'copse'," Arthur interrupted, "I take it you mean 'city'?"

"City," she tasted the unfamiliar word. She'd read it, of course, but as it connoted Bravenstadt in her mind, she had trouble relating it to the groves of trees that sheltered her people. Each Prandhaharan Copse was named for the dominant tree of its grove.

"I suppose you could apply that term," she agreed. "If you're using it to mean the place where many people have gathered to dwell."

Arthur looked puzzled. She rather liked that expression. His brow furrowed in a most endearing way. Much better than his usual haughty mien.

"What else would it mean?" he asked, with obvious sincerity.

"Well, as we don't use it at all, to me it's synonymous with 'Bravenstadt.' Which, of course, is nothing like a Prandhaharan copse."

He nodded, the cute little furrows clearing. "I see."

She turned from the path and led him to a willowy young sapling growing well away from its nearest neighbor.

"This is a banyan sapling," she said, reaching out to touch the trunk, no thicker than her forearm. "When it is grown, it will house several families. It is my job to influence its growth."

"Right," he said, his voice neutral, but his eyes registered his skepticism. "And how exactly do you accomplish that?"

She tamped down her indignation, not wanting to upset the infant tree. *He can't help it,* she told herself. *It's not his fault he's ignorant.*

With that comforting thought, she laid her hand flat against the supple young trunk and sought the banyan's spirit.

CHAPTER SIX

Arthur frowned. One minute the infuriating girl had been lecturing him on Prandhaharan government—something he was well aware of, having read up on the topic before leaving home!—and the next she'd wandered over to this puny little sapling and started spouting nonsense.

If it weren't for her undeniable beauty, which was much too immodestly displayed at the moment for his peace of mind—what well-bred young woman walked about in public in pants with her midriff exposed and her slender ankles so blatantly available to the common view?—he should send a pigeon to his father right now and request an autocarriage to convey him home to civilization.

He glanced at her again, couldn't seem to keep his gaze away from her lustrous hair, her shapely bosom, slender waist, firmly rounded hips. He licked his lips and pulled his gaze away from the ravishing creature before him.

Yes. She was beautiful. But her tongue! Her unseemly attitude! She was a harridan. Lovely to look at, but did he really want to saddle himself with such an outspoken shrew?

His traitorous eyes turned to her once again, and his mouth fell open.

Kanti stood perfectly still, the flat of her hand pressed against the spindly trunk of the little tree, eyes closed, and the tree...

Arthur scrubbed his hands over his face, rubbing his eyes carefully and thoroughly. He peered again at his betrothed. The vision hadn't changed. The little tree leaned toward the girl, its twig-like branches straining toward her, its bright green leaves trembling in their attempt to touch her.

He shook his head in disbelief, his gaze locked on the tableau.

Kanti stepped closer to the sapling and was enveloped in twigs and leaves. The tree caressed her face, petted her hair, trailed along her outstretched arm.

And the girl...her face glowed with contentment. No, that wasn't right. The air fairly hummed with emotion emanating from the unlikely pair.

Joy.

Pride.

Love!

Arthur stepped back, away from the alien sight, from the emotional shower he didn't, couldn't understand. He stopped, hand on chest as if to hold his racing heart in its place. Breathed deeply. He was here to retrieve his bride, but also to learn.

He didn't understand what was happening, but he could observe and record the experience.

He stepped toward Kanti, toward the alien creature with whom he'd pledged to spend his life. She was beautiful. She was intelligent, and she was undeniably communing with a tree.

His understanding of the world tilted. He would have to work to right it once more.

He hadn't yet decided whether or not to speak to her when he became aware of other presences. Turning, he found himself the focal point of three shining blades.

CHAPTER SEVEN

The sapling was agitated.

A frown touched Kanti's brow as she struggled to understand the young tree's concern. Not yet fully trained, the sapling had trouble marshaling its thoughts and presenting them to her in a coherent fashion. She waded through the impressions of breeze and birds, clouds and sunlight, and discovered men with swords.

Her eyes popped open and she turned to find Arthur facing three men who were indeed threatening him with swords! The men were clearly Prandhaharan, dressed as they were in loose white garments, their faces swathed in the trailing ends of their less than spotless turbans.

Whatever could they want?

As if in answer to her unspoken question, the middle man inclined his head to her and said, "We cannot allow Prince Misra to sell you to this Bravenstadt dog, Princess."

"It is not fitting that one with your gifts should be sent away to the heathens," added the second man.

The middle man addressed her again. "Leave now, Kanti

Misra. Go home to your father. Inform him that this wretch will trouble you no further."

"I will not," she said, putting as much imperious command in her voice as she could manage. "This man is a guest in my household. More than that, he is my betrothed husband. You dishonor our entire Copse with your actions."

The third man growled and stepped closer to Arthur, his blade coming closer to the young man's throat.

Her pulse raced, and as her hand dropped from the sapling's trunk, she lost her connection to the young tree's spirit. What could she do? How could she help?

She glanced at Arthur. The Bravenstadt man stood quite still, hands at his sides, chin slightly lowered. Except for a pulse-point beating on the side of his brow he seemed remarkably relaxed.

When he spoke, his voice was calm. "If you gentlemen intend that I should not see my betrothed again, please allow me to give her a memento."

Alarmed by his seeming acquiescence, Kanti sought the sapling's spirit. *Help me,* she sent. *Speak to your elders; tell them Kanti needs their help!*

The sapling jerked as though pelted with cold rain and acknowledged her distress.

The three men glanced at each other, but the leader shrugged. Clearly he could see no way this unarmed foreigner could foil their plans. "Bestow your token and then come with us." He turned a cold gaze on Kanti. "Do not make me hurt you, Princess. Accept his gift and leave."

She raised her chin and glared at the villain.

Arthur reached into his pocket. "Don't do anything foolish, my dear," he said as he withdrew his hand.

"Foolish! Why, you...you..." she spluttered.

Arthur grinned, and while the men's attention was riveted on his irritated betrothed he threw a small, etched metal ball into their midst.

The moment the ball left his hand it began to transform. Before it reached the nearest man, wings had sprouted, then a head and tail appeared and a colorful metallic bird began to sing in oddly echoing chirps and whistles as it soared around the men's heads.

The leader dropped his sword and batted at the bird in an attempt to protect his face.

The other two stumbled backward, making warding signs with their left hands, their right hands still holding their weapons, though laxly and without attention.

Arthur leapt into action. He delivered a forceful kick to the leader's right knee, dropping the man like a tree to an ax, then turned his fists on the second man.

Kanti joined the fray, punching and kicking the unwary third man, all the while screaming her fury.

The fight was short-lived. The two assailants still on their feet dropped their weapons and fled in face of the combined Prandhaharan and Bravenstadter fury, and the shouts of the prince's men as they ran to Kanti's aid.

She pushed a tendril of hair from her sweaty brow and smiled. The sapling had spread the alarm. The young tree had done well. Then she turned on Arthur, seeing him with new eyes.

"Foolish," she repeated, then smiled. "You used me as a distraction."

"I did," he said. "I may not be Prandhaharan, but I'm not stupid." He grinned and placed a sandal-shod foot on the neck of his would-be assassin. "I'm gratified to know that I gauged your reaction correctly."

She shook her head at his boldness and gazed into the sky where the mechanical bird still wheeled. "What is that thing?"

He followed her gaze and shrugged. "It's nothing," he said. "A mere bauble meant to amuse my bride."

"Well, I'm not amused," she said, looking deep into his eyes. "But I am very impressed."

He nodded and a serious expression flowed over his face. "I've misjudged you," he said quietly, "and I think you've misjudged me as well." He held out his hand. "Shall we begin again, and leave our prejudices behind?"

She cocked her head, raised an eyebrow, and then took his hand. Indeed. She had misjudged this man. He had courage. Dressed in unfamiliar clothes, in a foreign land, armed only with a pretty trinket and a rudimentary knowledge of her character, he had nonetheless acted with calm determination.

She was intrigued.

CHAPTER EIGHT

Prince Misra smiled. The plans he had laid with Bravenstadt industrialist Edvard Blakeslee had come to fruition. Following their adventure at the banyan sapling, Kanti and Arthur had determined to become acquainted, to give their betrothal a chance.

Their seedling relationship had grown over the last week and was now blossoming. Arthur now recognized Kanti's talents, and while he didn't claim to understand them, acknowledged their value. Kanti, for her part, had learned of Arthur's courage, intelligence, and wry humor. Had even come to believe that love might bloom between them.

Much to her father's delight, the young couple had made a few changes in the marriage contract. They would divide their time between Bravenstadt and Prandhahar, living in the industrialized city during fall and winter—the trees' dormant months—and in the Banyan Copse in spring and summer.

"And of course," Arthur said as he signed the amended document with a flourish, "while we're in Bravenstadt, you will dress appropriately."

"I'll what?" Kanti said, wide-eyed.

Arthur let his gaze slide over his willow-slim wife-to-be, appreciating her lovely curves. "Much as I enjoy the view, you'll cause autocarriage wrecks if you walk about Bravenstadt dressed like that!"

Kanti narrowed her eyes, but then glanced at her father's lifted brow and sighed. "Fine. I'll adopt Bravenstadt garb when I go out in public," she said, resigned, "but when at home and in our gardens, I shall dress as I please."

Arthur tapped his chin with a forefinger, and nodded. "Agreed."

Noting the finger on his chin, Kanti smiled. "One more thing," she murmured. "The facial hair must go. I won't be intimate with a man whose face makes me think of fuzzy caterpillars."

Arthur's face blazed red, then white, his hands flew protectively to his well-groomed beard and mustache. "Shave?" he gasped. "You expect me to shave?"

She met his gaze and smiled with as much promise as she could give without words. His Adam's apple bobbed and the pulse-point at his temple throbbed. He nodded, holding her gaze.

"As you wish, my lady," he murmured, taking her hand and brushing it with his lips.

Her eyes widened with surprise at the butterfly soft touch of his moustache.

Perhaps she'd have to rethink that last request...

ABOUT THE AUTHOR

Debbie Mumford specializes in speculative fiction—fantasy, paranormal romance, and science fiction. Author of the popular *Sorcha's Children* series, Debbie loves the unknown, whether it's the lure of space or earthbound mythology. She writes about dragon-shifters, ghostly detectives, and humanity's journey into the galaxy in tales of all lengths, from short stories to novels. Her work has been published in multiple volumes of *Fiction River*, as well as in *Heart's Kiss Magazine*, *Amazing Monster Tales: It Came From Outer Space*, and many other popular anthologies.

Learn more at:
www.debbiemumford.com.

facebook.com/DebbieMumfordWrites

THE LAST DEATH OF ANGFIL

KARI KILGORE

Maude Morgan loved autumn in Virginia City more than any other time. The worst of the hot Nevada days were past, the deepest cold of winter still distant. The constant, maddening wind dropped to the lowest it would be all year. An occasional rain relieved her skin from ever-present dryness, if only for a few moments.

Even the high mountains supplying the gold and silver fuel that drove Virginia City got in on the act, in their own way. The silvery green sagebrush that dotted the harsh desert bloomed yellow and orange. Maude smiled every time she caught the spicy, bitter scent on the newly gentle breeze.

Nothing compared to the rainy, constantly overcast months of her youth in Cornwall, England, to be sure. Or to the fiery oak, maple, and chestnut leaves now changing far to the east of this wild, vast continent. But autumn in the desert was a change to be enjoyed.

In all her lifetimes, Maude had learned to seek out and treasure change above all else.

The so-far endless riches of the nearby Comstock Lode in 1872 gave Maude both the means and the method to change her surroundings to suit her, aside from the weather. Her favorite ground floor room for meeting guests, clients, and allies alike shone with rich silks, fine velvet carpets, and the gleaming woodwork of her desk and emerald-green-upholstered furniture.

Visitors wandering into Maude's place of business off the bustling Main Street would have no doubt they were dealing with a woman of means, and they must act accordingly.

Men or women walking in quite on purpose—lost souls, business partners, or lives-long friends—knew they had arrived in precisely the right place.

Maude kept herself in the finest of fashions from Paris, San

Francisco, and the Orient, within reason. The vicious corsets were not to be tolerated, for example, and neither Maude nor any of the women who worked for her frequented dressmakers who insisted on using them. She welcomed the frontier's more relaxed profile of a long dress gathered at the waist. Today she wore a favorite in sapphire that brought out her pale English complexion and vivid blue eyes. Broad hats to protect her face from the fierce sun kept more than one milliner busy and well-paid.

Her current body had thirty-seven years, but all of Maude's study and practice with how her skin aged—and how to prevent it—allowed her to pass for much younger if need be.

The long, strangely mournful whistle of an arriving train broke the silence in the sitting room, and a young English woman entered before the echoes faded. Charlotte wore her chestnut hair down her back in a girlish braid rather than the elaborate head-topping arrangement Maude had to affect as a woman of her station.

The hair was the same color and texture, though, and the same heavy thickness. Charlotte was only one of several young women living in and around Virginia City who looked remarkably like Maude. Still others lived back in England, New York, Philadelphia, Chicago, everywhere Maude had settled long enough to make arrangements for their births and their care.

Everywhere she had passed a lifetime.

These precious young women and countless others before them served as Maude's heirs, her passage from one dying body to renewal in the next.

Charlotte, known to others as an unfortunate relative learning the ways of this strange new land, carried a beautifully carved and varnished wooden tray laid with a proper Cornish cream tea to mark the hour of four o'clock.

Tucked in around the freshly baked, fragrant scones, flowery delicate china pot of clotted cream, and matching pot of strawberry preserves, three tea cups waited rather than her usual one. Maude frowned at them before meeting Charlotte's gaze.

"Am I having company I have not been made aware of, Charlotte?"

Rather than quivering and getting fluttery and distressed at the question, Charlotte calmly carried on arranging the tea on a small oak table inlaid with gold and silver swirls and filigrees. Maude appreciated obedience, especially when living among so many unschooled and uncultured souls in this wild country.

She valued confidence in the manner of those around her even more.

"You are having company, ma'am," Charlotte said, her voice still holding the cultured accent of her London childhood. Maude did everything in her power to make sure her heirs were well educated. "Two gentlemen asking to see you."

Maude accepted her cup of hot tea, breathing in the bergamot fragrance.

"I don't recall Mr. Hannaford mentioning guests. As my social and business secretary, he truly should keep me informed of such arrangements."

This time Charlotte's cheeks colored the slightest bit as she arranged two extra plates on the table.

"The arrangement wasn't made through Mr. Hannaford, ma'am, but directly to me. From one of your associates in Chicago. A Mr. O'Day, with substantial holdings in lumber and shipping."

Maude raised her eyebrows and hummed to herself. This was a most interesting turn to an ordinary day. "What time are these two gentlemen expected?"

Charlotte straightened, smoothing her black skirts and small white apron.

"I asked them to set out when they heard the four o'clock

train arriving. Since they have rooms at a proper men's boarding house close by, that should be..." She smiled and tilted her head toward the bell ringing at the front door. "...any moment now, ma'am."

Maude didn't bother to hide her answering smile.

"Very well, Charlotte. You may see them in."

Mr. Robert O'Day—another like Maude with fine young heirs of his own—normally busied himself with his work. Since he coordinated massive shipments of lumber from Michigan, Wisconsin, and Minnesota into Chicago's great rail yards and throughout the continent, that was quite busy indeed.

In their many long years of association going back before the Romans to the origins of tin mining in Cornwall, Maude had never known Robert to be frivolous.

The two young men who trailed quietly behind Charlotte, broad hats in their hands, didn't look at all frivolous themselves. Both were black men, one tall and slender, the other shorter and more stocky, both with tightly curled hair cropped close against their skulls. They wore thigh-length brown jackets with high shirt collars underneath, old-fashioned by Eastern standards but typical of most men who could afford something other than work clothes in Virginia City.

"Mr. William Evans and Mr. Jacob Fairfax, ma'am," Charlotte said before she took up her place beside the tea service.

Maude nodded and waved her hand at the two curved wood and green chairs across from her.

"Mr. Evans, Mr. Fairfax. I'm pleased to make your acquaintance. Won't you join me in my afternoon refreshment?"

The men glanced at each other, their startlement clear, and Maude realized she knew nothing of their backgrounds. With the heartbreak and bitterness of a young country's war only a few years past, these two could be recently freed slaves or men born free outside the Confederacy. Or from outside the re-

United States altogether. Many such men worked in Virginia City and the other gold and silver boom towns throughout the West.

The shifts and resentments of the last decade, combined with Maude's years on the frontier, left her unsure of how to approach them.

Finally the smaller man returned her nod and stepped forward. His deep voice carried the lilt and music of the South.

"We surely do thank you for the offer, ma'am, but we don't want to be troubling you."

"It's no trouble at all, I assure you. Any friends of Mr. O'Day are friends of mine. I insist."

After another glance—this one seeming to carry more emotion and connection than Maude expected between the two —they sat and accepted cups of tea from Charlotte. Seeing everything proceeding normally, she curtseyed herself out of the room.

Maude noticed both men watching her slice her own scone in half, then add clotted cream and strawberry preserves to each half before doing the same to their own.

Strangers, then, at least to her imported English habits. Maude hadn't set foot in England or Europe since long before frequent tea consumption and the rituals surrounding it began. But updating up her habits and connections helped her fit in and belong, as well as disguising her truly ancient origins.

No one spoke until they had all enjoyed their scones.

"May I ask what brings you to Virginia City?" Maude said. "And how you're acquainted with Mr. O'Day?"

This time the taller man spoke, with no trace of his companion's Southern lilt.

"I'm sorry to say we've never met Mr. O'Day, ma'am, not face to face like we're sitting here with you. Mr. Evans and I traveled here from Chicago to find employment. Friends of his work with Mr. O'Day. They made the arrangements that led us to you."

The smaller man, Mr. Evans, put down his tea cup and retrieved a small envelope from his coat pocket. His hand trembled as he held it out toward Maude.

"We were told to hand this letter to you, ma'am." He swallowed, and his accent got even thicker. "I'm awful sorry to be so familiar, but I was told to ask for your help in a greatly peculiar way. *Mar pleg*, Miss Meraud."

Maude's breath caught, and her teacup clattered as she set it down. Mr. Evans' way of speaking almost added another syllable to her ancient birth name, *Mer*-aud-uh. And his pronunciation of *Please* in the nearly forgotten Cornish language was dreadful.

But he never could have known to say such things in any accent unless Robert O'Day or someone close to him had explained it.

"My goodness," Maude said. "You have certainly livened up my day, Mr. Evans, Mr. Fairfax." She took the envelope, and now her hand trembled as well. "If you'll please excuse me, I expect I'll learn why in this letter."

The heavy, cream-colored paper was still sealed with a neat circle of one half red, one half green wax. Maude admired Robert's technique, and his clever use of both colors that marked this correspondence as private. She snapped his elaborate initials in half and flattened the folded square out into a page covered with his close, precise handwriting in a language only a handful of people in the world remembered.

My dearest friend,

I humbly beg your assistance on behalf of these two gentlemen. Through no fault of his own, Mr. Evans has run afoul of a man from both our pasts. A man we might both wish dead and removed from this earth, if only that were a possibility. It appears he has named himself George Winters for this lifetime, and that he lives it as foully as he has all his others.

You remember the harsh treatment of the Cornish, Welsh, and Irish in our distant homeland, as well as how such vile behavior gave our Mr. Winters joy and twisted satisfaction. You and I both witnessed this firsthand during the time of the Romans, and we were both lucky enough to have the means to leave our homelands rather than become victims ourselves.

I have recently learned Mr. Winters also gleefully involved himself in the despicable slave trade that brought ancestors of Mr. Evans and other poor souls to these shores. To put it mildly, Mr. Winters has not taken kindly to the resolution of the conflict, and the resulting freedom for the suffering.

He has since made it his mission to track down and murder the former captives from one of his plantations. He has been cruel, methodical, and successful in his quest. I expect he will continue on to hunt down the freed from other plantations if given the opportunity.

Mr. Evans is unfortunately his current target.

I feel those of our kind bear some responsibility for Mr. Winters. And our kind alone have the means and knowledge to stop him before he succeeds yet again.

I regret that Mr. Winters has been allowed to make it to your base of operations in the West. I ask that you please assist in this grave task, my dear Meraud, and bring your considerable powers into play.

I shall depart Chicago tomorrow to join you, and I and all of my heirs and allies stand ready to assist however we may.

Yours with love and respect as always,

John O'Day

Maude folded the letter, tucked it into a pocket of her skirt, and picked up her cooled tea.

"May I ask how you became aware of the threat to your life, Mr. Evans?"

He stared down at his hands knotted in his lap, and Maude would have sworn a flush rose against his dark skin.

"I heard tell of the murder of friends of mine," he said. "From before. Friends from the bad days, back in Georgia. Murdered in Richmond, and Philadelphia, and New York. Then Chicago, and St. Louis, and Denver. It was one of Jacob's people that got word of what Mr. O'Day knew, after we got out here to Virginia City a week past."

Mr. Fairfax—Jacob—gazed at Mr. Evans with a fondness Maude finally recognized and understood. These two weren't simply friends or traveling companions. They meant far more to each other than that.

Mr. Fairfax confirmed her suspicions with his words and the heat of his tone.

"The things William told me about his life...before, they aren't fit for a lady to hear, ma'am. I'll do *anything* in my power to make sure he's safe from harm. That man that's after him, Mr. Winters. He's the very devil in the flesh."

Maude nodded, doing her best to keep her own voice steady.

"He is that, Mr. Fairfax. He is that. Have either of you seen Mr. Winters here, in Virginia City? Or should I ask if you've ever met him, to know what he may look like?"

The question wasn't an idle one. Maude knew many of her kind changed their appearances as much as they were able in dangerous times, with varying degrees of success.

Mr. Winters was particularly good at disguise.

Mr. Evans slowly shook his head.

"I don't believe I ever laid eyes on him, ma'am. Not unless it was before, in Georgia. But I lived in that same spot since I was a boy and saw more people than I could ever bring to mind, so he might stand right in front of me and I'd never know."

Mr. Fairfax shook his head as well.

"Well then," Maude said, "I shall have to bring the two of

you to live here, under my protection. I'll call my social secretary to make the arrangements to bring your things. Mr. Winters is not an enemy to take lightly, so I won't have you walking the streets."

Both men stared at her, their smooth, dark brows wrinkled and their eyes worried.

"We just both found employment two days ago, ma'am," Mr. Fairfax said. "Loading up the waste out of the mine to be carried off. If we don't show up tomorrow, they'll let us go."

Maude nodded. "They will indeed. I assure you, between Mr. O'Day and myself, we will find you better work at a better wage. If not here, then with one of Mr. O'Day's railroad companies. In the meantime, you're welcome to get settled in your rooms upstairs."

She got to her feet, and a few seconds later both men stood. Mr. Evans glanced at Mr. Fairfax before he spoke to Maude.

"Last thing I'd want in the world is for you to have trouble with this Mr. Winters, ma'am. Least of all for trying to help me. Or trouble with your neighbors for keeping men such as us."

Maude started to tell them she had strong guards and plenty of them, and then she caught the way they wouldn't meet her gaze.

No, this wasn't only worry about her safety, at least not from Mr. Winters. And not only about a white woman sheltering black men, either.

So many layers to consider, even before she faced the true danger at hand.

"I understand, Mr. Evans. I appreciate the word of warning, I truly do. Coming from back East, you may not be aware of the custom of bachelor marriages prevalent in the West. Neither Mr. O'Day nor I will worry ourselves about that. As for my neighbors, they learned well years ago that I can permit or block items they dearly need, such as lumber shipping through Chicago and other vital supplies. They also learned well to tend to their own business rather than mine."

Maude rang the tiny silver bell she rarely used to summon Charlotte or anyone else. Anyone who heard it knew the matter was of the highest importance.

"Now please, let Charlotte help you get settled, and let me worry about Mr. Winters. I've known more of his crimes and sins than you can possibly imagine. I'll take great care, I promise."

~

Hours later, after asking Mr. Hannaford to cancel her appointments for the next few days, consulting with her mortal allies in Virginia City, and a quiet supper with Mr. Evans and Mr. Fairfax, Maude again entertained two guests in her ground floor study.

Both as long-lived as she, and as eager to protect their comfortable lives in the West from interference or danger from their pasts.

Walter Bergman, owner of one of the largest mining outfits in Nevada, long known to Maude from their origins in Cornwall. The two of them came to the New World with the discovery of iron ore in the 1600s, bringing experienced Cornish miners and the fortunes to build the new industry. They'd crossed the great land together with each new discovery of underground riches.

He sprawled in his chair, more comfortable and relaxed than his formal black coat and pants would allow for anywhere else. His shoulder-length brown hair was fairly clean but mussed, and his beard and moustache were in dire need of a good trim.

Isobelle Fenywick, Madam of the most respected brothel in Virginia City, and of similar establishments in larger mining towns and cities throughout the continent. She brought her centuries of experience in Europe to serve the Continental Army in the 1700s, along with her fierce protectiveness of the women who worked for her.

As always, Isobelle wore a ruby red gown far more fashionable and expensive than any of Maude's. Her exquisitely small-waisted figure and upright posture reflected the iron grip of her corset. The golden curls framing her heart-shaped face somehow looked fresh and new so late into the evening.

Like Maude, Walter and Isobelle had brought several of their heirs on the dangerous voyage across the Atlantic Ocean, then took care to establish them in various cities as they moved West. Everyone of their kind bore children who had the right body type—children of the same sex they could move into and have new life—about half the time. Luckily *all* of their same-sex children could in turn bear the right ones later on.

Like Maude, Isobelle depended on her female children to do the dangerous and tedious work of producing new heirs. Walter, of course, had no such difficulties. He made sons as easily as his sons did.

And like most of their kind, they protected each other, and built and reinforced that protection together.

Isobelle sipped French brandy from her sparkling crystal glass, then focused on Maude. Her accent in this life was also French, and even though Maude knew it was fake, Isobelle was as skilled as the rest of them in such things.

"But why would you risk so much for men such as these? Robert O'Day is wrong to ask such things of you, Maude."

"I've never known Robert to be wrong in his understanding of people," Maude said. "I've spoken to Mr. Evans and Mr. Fairfax, and I believe them to be good men. Gentle men, if not gentlemen. We have a greater obligation as well because of Mr. Winters. He cannot be allowed to roam free in the New World as he did in the old."

Walter held up his brandy before draining it. His gruff voice and rough words suited Virginia City as much as his faint aroma of sweat and unwashed body did.

"Hear-hear! That blasted man's been a curse on humanity for as long as I've been living, and that's too damn long for my liking. I don't much care what you or Robert Whatever-he's-calling-himself in Chicago have to say, or what kind of men you got sleeping in your upstairs room. Pardon me for saying so, but I call this Mr. Winters by his ancient name of Angfil and no other. If there's odds long or short on getting rid of that devil, I'm your man."

"And neither of you have seen or heard of Angfil being here?" Maude said. "In Virginia City?"

Isobelle shuddered, then shook her head.

"Not a whisper of it. This Mr. Winters has never been the kind to want to visit my girls, though, or to be allowed to. I have often heard his tastes run to...rougher pleasures than I would ever condone. I might not recognize him if I did have the misfortune of seeing him after so long."

"Not a word to my ears," Walter said. "Or my eyes. He never was an honest working man that I heard of. None of the short-lifers knew anything, Maude?"

Maude held up her glass to the gas lamp beside her, examining the honey-colored liquid inside.

"No mortal has heard of him or seen him, not that I can tell. You know as well as I do how easily he changes his looks. We'll have to draw him out. He'll be down at the poorest of cribs, out past the Chinese section of town. Preying on girls who can't afford the protection someone like you brings, Isobelle."

"He never kills them, the girls," Isobelle said. "That would be too easy, too quick for him. He may well be terrorizing the Chinese for *that* purpose, knowing no one will protect them."

Maude closed her eyes, bringing to her mind the last time she'd faced Mr. Winters.

Angfil.

Not long before she'd taken her leave of England forever.

Hidden away in the craggy granite heights of the moors, sheltered by fog. Watching Angfil slaughter and slash his way through brave fighters below, with superior force and strange weapons, unknown tactics brought from Europe.

Screaming and laughing his joy.

Surrounded by dozens of his own heirs, giving himself a most twisted gift of fighting, dying, and taking a new body over and over and over again.

His features and form had been forever branded in her memory that day.

She opened her eyes, finished her brandy, and poured herself another.

"I would recognize him, despite his skill at disguise. And *my* skill at disguise will make certain no one in the cribs or Chinese section will recognize me. This is what we will do."

~

Late into that same night, Maude walked—or more honestly she shuffled—along the row of pitiful cribs on the outskirts of Virginia City. No sturdy brick or even solid wooden structures here, so distant from the fine Main Street.

Barely worthy of being called shacks, the flimsy dwellings stood shoulder to shoulder, none of them much taller than Maude herself. Clearly built from scrap wood scavenged from the rapid, non-stop construction in town, none of the boards seemed to match in width or color. Makeshift porches made of more scrap or even canvas stretched in front of some, along with rickety chairs a fierce desert wind would turn into kindling.

Maude was a thousand times thankful for the heavy miner's boots that gave her some protection from the filth underfoot.

Her nose and watering eyes told her the mucky spots she saw by her the weak lamplight weren't damp from the scant rain.

Her hunched over, labored gait helped her blend in with more people moving about than she'd expected, as did the dark and tattered work dress and shawl over her hair. Sporting women leaving for work or returning stood out in their white gowns, but many men and women looked like Maude. A general low roar of voices swirled and rose and fell around her.

Several steps ahead, dressed in similar threadbare and unwashed clothing, Mr. William Evans walked alone.

Maude knew her mining friend Walter Bergman was nearby, along with several guards. They'd likely be the only ones with guns in this destitute underworld, and they would never let her or William out of their sight.

She'd listened as William and Jacob Fairfax talked it over and decided the risk was worth it. They'd agreed this was likely the only way to draw out the devil who had followed William and so many others all the way from Georgia.

And still, she was badly frightened for William, even more than for herself. She kept seeing the terror in Jacob's eyes when they'd said goodbye.

As she had countless times throughout her many lifetimes, Maude wished she could sense others of her kind nearby. She'd heard of many with that skill. She'd never felt her own lack as keenly as she did in that moment.

A commotion and disturbance in the crowd to her right warned her, almost too late.

A hulking shadow flowed through like water, nearly impossible to see. He darted and seemed to disappear like a cat on the prowl, with a living, breathing human being his prey.

Maude gripped the gutting knife hidden in the folds of her dirty skirt and moved closer to William.

A hulking man to match the shadow stepped into their path,

grinning like the devil himself. Lank hair fell well past his shoulders, and a matted growth of beard hid his face.

But Maude knew.

This man *was* the devil.

Angfil.

"I believe you belong to me, boy."

William backed up fast, exactly as they'd planned.

Angfil closed faster than they'd expected, wrapping one long arm around William's neck.

"You gonna tell me you don't recognize me? After all I did for you, and for so long?"

Maude ran around behind him, drawing her deadly and experienced blade.

She stood on her toes and held it to Angfil's throat, heedless of the danger to herself.

"*I* recognize you, Angfil," she nearly growled. "Your days of terrorizing the weak have come to an end."

He threw his head back and laughed, pushing his greasy, reeking hair into Maude's face.

"I don't recognize *you*, and I don't give a damn who you are. Slice away, little girl. I'm a ghost in the flesh of your worst nightmare. I'll track this boy down and come back for you next."

Maude shouted at William as she yanked the knife toward her and across, the hot splash and metallic reek of his blood pouring over her hand.

"Run!"

Angfil's laughter never faltered, that was the hell of it. Even as he sagged to his knees, pulling Maude down with him, it still gurgled out of his dying body.

Only when she saw William disappear into the gathering crowd did Maude stagger up and away from the monster face down in the filth.

A hand grabbed her arm, and she barely stopped herself

from slashing her bloody knife that way. A black woman stared into Maude's eyes.

"You got to get out of here, miss," she said, her voice low and musical. "A storm of trouble about to break right here, bad enough that the law will surely notice."

Maude shook her head, trying to scan the faces all around for Angfil's heirs. He didn't have long, probably less than half an hour, before his spirit would be trapped in his dead flesh and unable to transfer.

Forever.

"No, we have to get *him* out of here," she said. "We can't let anyone take him."

She spotted Walter shoving his way through the thick crowd then, and she let herself sag against the woman who still held tight to her arm.

"No ma'am," the woman said, shaking her head. "This one already murdered his last. Stand up tall and look around you now."

Maude saw Walter stop, his eyes wide and jaw dropped.

She let the woman pull her upright and turned.

Someone shoved a limp body forward, toward Angfil. A body with the same build and the same face, clean-shaven and years younger.

One of Angfil's heirs.

By the time Walter made it to Maude's side, three more bodies landed on top of the first two. Years older and gray, the same age and bald. One with his hair dyed blond. All different enough that a mortal would never notice.

And every one another heir.

Maude stared at the black woman still standing beside her.

"I don't understand. How did you know? How did any of you know?"

The woman nodded once and bowed low.

"Miss Gertrude Hopewell, at least in this lifetime. Glad to meet you, Miss Maude Morgan."

Six dead men now lay at their feet.

"But how..." Maude whispered.

Gertrude turned to Walter. "Can you tell who I am, or at least *what* I am, Mr. Walter Bergman?"

Walter nodded as he took Gertrude's hand.

"You're one of us," he said. "Miss Gertrude, ma'am."

"That I am, sir. Now will you take these evil things away with you? Bury them at the bottom of the deepest mine you have? Close as you can get them to hell?"

"Yes ma'am. I surely will. I'll see that it's done, and I'll get Miss Maude and Mr. Evans away from here."

Gertrude bowed again, only her head this time. Then she let go of Maude and Walter and stood proud and tall.

"I thank you, as the wide world thanks you. Now away with you, and be well."

~

LATE THE NEXT MORNING, Maude poured herself another cup of the strong coffee Walter and so many others in the West preferred over tea. The flavor was harsh for her taste, even with thick cream and plenty of sugar.

This morning at least, she admitted she needed it.

Walter sat with her, keeping pace with his own coffee, making liberal use of her sugar. Maude expected Isobelle for their late brunch, along with a special guest yet to arrive, and she hoped Mr. Evans and Mr. Fairfax would be down in time to join them.

If not, she'd send Charlotte up with plenty of food for a lover's reunion to last the whole morning and afternoon long.

Walter still hadn't shaved or had a trim, but he had managed to wash his hair and put on clean clothes. The coffee wasn't doing anything to hide the weary shadows under his eyes. Maude feared she looked the same.

Rather than passing for younger, a stranger might take her for older than she was today.

"Did you ever find out who she was?" Walter said. "Miss Gertrude, I mean. Where she came from?"

"No. Not a word so far. Neither Mr. Evans nor Mr. Fairfax know, and no one down at the cribs seemed to, either. Or maybe they simply aren't talking."

"That may be just as well, Maude. We don't live in a world where a black woman can cause the death of one white man and live. Much less several of them. All of our kind guard their secrets. Sometimes even from each other."

Maude considered for a moment, and decided she had to ask. Even if she was afraid of the answer.

"Do you know what will happen to Angfil? Down in that mine, trapped in his dead body?"

Walter shrugged. "I know what I've heard. Some say he'll stay there for all eternity, unless someone manages to set him free. They say that hasn't happened for thousands of years, though. No one seems to know how anymore."

"He said he was a ghost," Maude said, almost to herself. "That's what I've heard. If we're trapped like that, we can't ever die. Even if we want to. We can only turn into ghosts and haunt the living."

Walter shuddered, and Maude couldn't hide her smile.

"He'd be a particularly nasty one. That shaft he's in and everything around it was already played out. Got men filling it in right now with junk and tailings." He scrubbed his hands through his hair, leaving it full of static and standing on end. "What time does our friend Robert O'Day arrive?"

The lonesome whistle of an arriving train echoed through Virginia City.

"If the telegram Charlotte gave me this morning was accurate," Maude said, "that would be his train. With my new shipment of brandy since I mysteriously seem to be running short. He'll find his way down Main Street to us in time for brunch. And we'll all raise a glass to the last death of Angfil."

ABOUT THE AUTHOR

Kari Kilgore's lifelong habit of expecting strange and wonderful things around every corner provides especially fertile ground for storytelling.

She started her first published novel *Until Death* in Transylvania, Romania, and finished it in Room 217 at the Stanley Hotel in Estes Park, Colorado, where a rather famous creepy tale about a hotel sparked into life. That's just one example of how real world inspiration drives her fiction. While her wanderlust and imagination lead her all over the world on grand adventures, her heart and family bring her home to her native Appalachian Mountains of Virginia.

Kari's stories have appeared in *Fiction River* anthology magazine, as well WMG Publishing's Holiday Spectacular edited by Kristine Kathryn Rusch. Kari's mystery stories are regularly featured in *Mystery, Crime, and Mayhem* Magazine.

Kari writes fantasy, science fiction, romance, mystery, contemporary fiction, and everything in between. She's happiest when she surprises herself. She lives at the end of a long dirt road in the middle of the woods with her husband Jason A. Adams, various house critters, and wildlife they're better off not knowing more about.

For more information about Kari, upcoming publications, her travels and adventures, and The Confidential Adventure Club, visit www.karikilgore.com.

LIKE OUR FATHERS BEFORE US

ANNIE REED

The dust storm chased Beau off the street and into the first open business he came to, an unremarkable saloon in yet another town with a name like Last Chance or Dry Gulch or Desperation. If this town even had a name.

Beau had visited more than his share of places like this during the time he'd spent in the world of men. Each time he hoped that when his job was done, he could finally return home to the land of the elves, a place that was lush and green and filled with so much magical life that the very ground seemed to have a life of its own. He'd spent far too much of his long, long life in places where the very air tasted like dry, lifeless dirt, but there was always one more spirit to rescue, one more evil, greedy man to punish.

He brushed the dust off his long coat and knocked it off his hat. He wiped an arm across his face to get the dust away from his eyes, but he didn't bother to clean the dirt away from the rest of his skin.

Unlike the men who sat in the saloon nursing their drinks, Beau had no beard and never would. Where their skin was rough and scarred by long hours spent underground working in the mines, his skin was smooth and unblemished. His jaw was square and strong, but his nose was narrow and delicate, almost feminine, and his eyes were a brilliant, piercing blue.

He'd learned long ago that the wide brim of his hat and the dirt on his face helped to camouflage the oddness of his features, just like his long, unkempt hair hid his most striking difference—the gently pointed tips of his ears. His filthy appearance made him look like any other weary traveler, and most men, like the men hunched over their drinks or playing cards while they waited out the storm, didn't give him a second glance.

The saloon consisted of a single, low-ceilinged room, large

enough to hold a few rough-hewn tables and chairs and the dozen or so men within. A plank board stretched across two barrels in the back served as a bar. Lanterns were hung from the ceiling at irregular intervals, and more lanterns sat on the bar.

The warm lantern light softened the hard edges of the place, but no one would ever mistake the saloon for anything than what it was: a place where broken men could come to drink and escape the hopelessness of their lives, at least for a little while.

Places like this hurt Beau's heart.

Life didn't have to be this way.

The mining country of the west was a hard land, full of high deserts and higher mountains with jagged peaks and treacherous canyons. The men who worked the mines had come to the west with dreams of riches, dreams few of them would ever realize. Yet they still dug deeper and deeper into the earth, chasing an ever-elusive goal.

Beau knew half a dozen spells that would tell them exactly where to dig to tap into a rich vein. He knew beings that could sniff out underground rivers that would turn towns like this into an oasis.

But the use of magic in the world of men was strictly forbidden, and those laws were enforced by wizards.

Men, the wizards declared, weren't ready to accept the widespread existence of magic folk, so elves like Beau along with all the other magic folk who'd existed since time began kept to themselves. If men learned the extent of the magical world that co-existed with their own, if they understood the power that magic users wielded, they would become frightened of anyone who commanded such power. What men feared, they hated.

And what they hated, they soon destroyed.

Of course, just like in the world of men, some magical folk thought the rules did not apply to them.

The old gods in particular had flaunted the rules. The old

gods, Beau's father had told him, were for the most part petty and vain and impossible to control, even for the wizards. A truce had finally been declared to prevent all-out war between the wizards and the old gods. As long as the old gods limited their interaction with men to those who worshipped them, the wizards agreed to leave them alone.

Only the wizards hadn't counted on the extent to which the old gods coveted more and more worshippers in the world of men. The more worshippers the gods had, the greater their power in the world. Their vanity and thirst for power inevitably led them to battle each other, with men as the ultimate prize.

The old gods had finally tired of war and the constant battles for power. They abandoned the world for new homes in the night sky where they could be adored from afar. Their worshippers, deprived of the attention of the gods whom they had adored, turned to passing down tales of the gods from generation to generation, embellishing each tale with subsequent retellings. Eventually those stories became more myth than truth, more legend than reality.

From time to time, other magic folk became careless about hiding themselves from the world of men, and new legends were born.

Magic folk who lived in the deep seas didn't understand that men had no means to protect themselves from the sensual pleasures those creatures exuded because that was their nature. Tales grew of sirens and mermaids who had the power to entrance men, and with each retelling, new legends were born.

Changelings who took the shape of great beasts simply to enjoy the thrill of the hunt or the sensory overload of running through a virgin forest under a full moon never realized that their metamorphosis gave rise to tales of werewolves and skinwalkers.

Beau was sure that if he wasn't careful, at some point in time men would tell tales of a tall, thin man with delicate features, piercing blue eyes, and pointed ears who could run like the wind and walk on the snow without leaving a single footprint behind. What legends would arise about him with each subsequent retelling? That his beauty hid a murderous monster who could kill with a mere touch?

There were times when Beau felt that such legends wouldn't be far from the truth. There were nights like tonight that he felt like the worst monster who had ever walked the earth.

He'd hoped he could take care of his business quietly. That the moonless night would hide his dark work so that no man would see him, but the dust storm had driven everyone—including Beau—inside.

He was a lawgiver like his father before him. But unlike the lawmen of the west who wore stars on their vests and delivered justice with a six-gun, Beau performed his duties as directed by the talisman he carried. A talisman that contained powerful magics.

When Beau first took his oath as a lawgiver and was given his talisman, the talisman allowed him a certain amount of discretion on how he used its magics, either to subdue or to kill the evil, greedy men he'd been sent to find. But as the long years wore on, the talisman's notion of justice had turned cold and deadly, as if the evil in the men he chased had infected the talisman itself. Tonight the talisman had given Beau no discretion at all.

He no longer wore the talisman on a leather strap around his neck. The deadly weight of the talisman had taken a toll on Beau's own spirit. What had seemed like a necessary duty when he'd first been given custody of the black stone and its magics had become an almost unbearable burden.

He carried it now in the pocket of his long coat, where it

burned with an intensity that told him the spirit he sought was indeed inside this unremarkable saloon.

Beau wanted to throw the talisman into the night. Let the dust storm destroy it. Let the windblown sand scrub the magics from its black face and leave it to fend for itself in the desert wasteland. Even if he was banished from his home for failing to carry out this night's work, the last of his duties as a lawgiver, he wanted to be rid of the talisman once and for all.

For if he used it this night—if he did what the talisman insisted be done—Beau would be taking the life of his oldest friend.

~

When compared to the lifespans of men, elves would have seemed nearly immortal. Beau himself had been alive before the first men from Europe crossed the great ocean to the east and landed on the shores of the continent that Beau and his kin called home.

He hadn't seen the event himself. He'd been a young elf then, barely more than a child. He lived with the rest of his kin, hundreds of them, in a great forest that stretched from the low rolling hills in the east to the great lakes to the northwest. A place of tall trees and thick meadows and lands teeming with magical folk. The land had been only sparsely populated by men who, for the most part, lived in harmony with the land.

It had been a wonderful time to be alive. The magical folk who lived in the forest had no great need to hide themselves. They lived out in the open and communed with other magical beings as easily as men breathed air.

This was the world as it existed before the greedy, murderous men arrived from the sea, bringing with them magical beings they had enslaved and forced to do their bidding.

Their arrival was communicated to Beau's kin by the spirit trees.

The spirits who lived in the trees had existed since before the last ice age. They'd hidden deep underground to survive the onslaught of the horrid cold, and many had perished while they waited for the land to warm again.

When the ice finally receded and the first trees sprouted from the remains of their ancestors, the spirits flocked to the new trees. The trees provided a safe haven for the spirits, and in return, the spirits sang to the trees, encouraging them to grow tall and strong.

The spirit trees flourished within the great forests of the east. Their gentle songs made the land more fertile and imbued the living with well-being and contentment. They communicated with each other over vast distances, and freely shared the information they obtained with other magic folk like Beau and his kin.

The men who came from across the sea focused their greedy eyes on the spirit trees. They realized that enslaving these gentle spirits would give them far greater power over their fellow man than the magical folk they'd enslaved to ensure safe passage for their ships.

These greedy men had come to this new world intending to rule its lands, and they'd been ready to kill to achieve their goal. But when they learned that the spirit trees exerted a magic that could influence men, they realized the land could be conquered with far less effort than they'd originally anticipated.

So with the help of the magical folk who'd protected their ships from the seas, these evil, greedy men tricked the spirit trees. They offered the gentle spirits an opportunity to see more of the world, exotic places the evil men had traveled and already plundered. Even though the spirits had lived long, long lives, they were naïve. They failed to see the evil behind the invaders' friendly, false smiles. Too many of the gentle spirits agreed, for they were curious to see the world beyond the forests in which they lived.

Only afterwards did these spirits realize that the only way to travel was for their trees to be slaughtered, which trapped the spirits inside, enslaved now to the will of the greedy, evil men who had tricked them.

Beau's kin were sworn protectors of the great forests. When word of the spirit trees' enslavement reached the elves and word of the misuse of magic by men reached the wizards who controlled such things, Beau and his kin were sent to free the spirits from the mutilated remains of their trees. Each swore an oath as a lawgiver, and each was given a talisman to use to not only free the spirits but also to mete out justice to the enslavers.

Over the decades, Beau had freed countless spirits who'd been imprisoned in the objects created from the corpses of their trees. Most had been grateful. Some, still mourning the death of the trees in which they'd lived, hadn't wanted to leave, and it had been Beau's duty to encourage them.

The most misused among them had been driven insane.

Beau had encountered one such spirit in his travels. Upon its release from the wooden crate which had been crafted from the spirit's tree, the spirit had turned on its enslaver with a viciousness that had shocked Beau to his core.

The spirit had held Beau at bay, and even with his great strength, Beau had been unable to break free. Instead he'd been forced to watch as the enraged spirit attacked its enslaver, inflicting so much pain and suffering on the greedy man that he'd fled into the night, a gibbering, slobbering, flayed creature condemned to spend what few years of his life that remained in a never-ending nightmare of his own creation.

Once the spirit had exacted its revenge, it allowed the talisman to pass judgment on it. The talisman's judgment had been harsh and final. The spirit was to be destroyed.

Beau had watched with a heavy heart as the spirit's energy flared briefly and then dissipated into the night as if it had never lived at all.

He had burned the remains of its tree, keeping watch over the fire until the flames consumed the last of the crate.

From that night on, the talisman had demanded that all spirits Beau tracked be destroyed, not simply freed, and that their enslavers be killed as well. Any discretion Beau might have had in the matter no longer existed, and his life became one of delivering death.

The spirit Beau had tracked to this saloon had been imprisoned far longer than the spirit who'd been driven insane.

It had been his friend when he'd been a boy. A kind and gentle being who'd allowed Beau to lounge on the branches of its tree so they could both stare at the sky, laugh at the chattering birds who built nests among the leaves, and call out the names of shapes they saw in the clouds.

And now he would have to destroy it. The talisman had given him no alternative.

As for the enslaver, Beau wouldn't need the talisman's magics to mete out justice to such a greedy, evil man.

Beau would take care of that himself.

∼

The enslaver was not what Beau had expected.

Men aged much more rapidly than elves, and Beau had been a lawgiver for a very long time. Most of the enslavers he'd tracked were old and frail by the time Beau found them and released the spirits they had enslaved.

A few of those men had learned how to force the spirits to use their magical power to enhance their enslaver's vitality and longevity. Those enhanced men moved from place to place when it became evident they didn't age like normal men. It was one of the many ways Beau found them.

But even men who'd abused the spirits' energies to elongate their lives still aged. Splotches of color the shade of old leather marred their skin. Their hair turned brittle and wispy, their spines bent and fragile. Their large-knuckled fingers twisted into weak claws barely able to hold a tin cup of whiskey, much less draw and fire a gun.

Only their eyes retained a touch of the vitality they'd stolen from the spirits. Their eyes told the story of men who knew they were facing the end of their long, long lives, and there was nothing more they could do to stop death from claiming them.

The enslaver in this no-name saloon was none of those things.

He was young and slender, his beard barely evident on his smooth skin, his dark hair almost as long as Beau's own. He sat on a bench by himself off to one side of the bar, a tin cup on the table in front of him, and a battered guitar at his side.

The talisman in Beau's pocket burned when he turned his gaze on the guitar.

The tree in which Beau's spirit friend had lived had been tall and magnificent. Its branches reached wide and strong. Whatever else had happened to the tree after the enslaver had killed it and mutilated its corpse, the guitar was the last bit of the dead tree which still imprisoned Beau's spirit friend.

And it was this young man's proudest possession.

Beau could tell by the way he kept one hand on the guitar as it lay on the bench beside him. The way his fingers, as slender as Beau's own, gently touched the strings and stroked the wood.

Beau bought a whiskey from the bartender and took it over to the young man's table.

"A song for a drink?" he asked, holding the tin cup of whiskey out toward the young man.

Beau was careful to keep the brim of his hat tilted down to keep his eyes in shadow, but he still felt a jolt as the young man lifted his gaze to meet Beau's. Whether this man knew it or not, he had a touch of magic about him that had nothing to do with the enslaved spirit in the guitar.

"You want a song with this storm and all?" The young man gave a rueful shake of his head. "I wouldn't mind a drink if you're offering, but you ain't gonna hear much of what you're paying for." He stroked the strings so softly they barely made a sound. "I don't play her hard, mister. She's a lot older than I am."

The storm chose that moment to howl its fury, rattling the saloon's door in its frame as the wind whistled through the cracks in the walls, bringing dust with it.

"Then you mind if I sit for a spell?" Beau asked. "It looks to be a long night."

The young man nodded at the bench on the opposite side of the table, and Beau sat down.

"The guitar must be very special to you," Beau said. "I didn't expect to see such a fine instrument in a place like this."

The young man snorted. "Fine instrument? She was at one time, that's for sure, back when my granddaddy played her. My pa used to say that granddaddy made her himself, a present for my gran, but I think he was pulling my leg. Granddaddy never made no other guitars, no instruments of any kind. Mostly he just carved toys for us kids, you know? But this guitar, he sure treated her fine."

He picked up the guitar and cradled it on his lap almost like a lover. Beau could see the remnants of the polish that must have made the guitar gleam as satiny soft as a rose petal when it was new.

The guitar was well loved, that much was clear. It had been crafted with care, not with a greedy or evil intent.

The spirit still lived inside the guitar's old wood. Beau could feel its presence. Trapped inside, it couldn't communicate with him the same way they had when Beau had climbed the branches of its tree, but he still felt...

Joy?

Happiness?

How could that be?

How could a spirit enslaved and forced to use its magics at the whim of its enslaver be happy?

"It reminds me of a friend I knew long ago," Beau said.

The young man beamed at him. "You know, that's what my gran used to say. That the guitar was like an old friend." He squinted his eyes, peering at Beau's face. "You look a little like her, especially around the eyes. Pa said I took after her side of the family. I know I got the same eyes as her. Now wouldn't it be something if it turned out we was related. I ain't got no family left hereabouts since Pa was killed in the mines."

Beau started to shake his head, then he stopped himself.

Could they be related, if only in a very distant way?

The young man—and he was only a man—had a touch of magic about him. Men did not possess magic. Not unless they had an ancestor who'd been magical.

It was rare but not totally unheard of for magical folk to fall in love with someone from the world of men. What if Beau wasn't the first to find his old spirit friend? Had this young man's grandmother been a lawgiver like Beau? It wasn't out of the question.

What seemed impossible was that a lawgiver could have fallen in love with an enslaver. Beau had been told that the enslavers were evil, greedy men. That the punishments these men suffered were their just rewards for the wrongs they had done to the spirit trees.

That when he allowed the talisman's magics to kill them, he'd been doing the right thing.

But what he'd been wrong?

What if some of these men had been kind?

What if some of them had treated the spirits as well as they could once they discovered what they had done?

"Does your granddaddy still make toys?" Beau asked.

"You know, I don't rightly know." The young man's fingers formed a chord on the guitar's neck and his other hand plucked the strings. "One day a stranger came to town, and he and my grandma up and disappeared. I'd always hoped he'd come back someday since he left his guitar behind, but he never did."

Beau heard the words and understood their hidden meaning—the former lawgiver and this man's grandaddy had been discovered living among men, and they'd fled to protect not only themselves but their kin—but his attention was riveted on the guitar.

Underlying the soft, pure tones the strings produced was an unspoken language that Beau knew well.

He'd heard it in his mind when he'd been just a boy, when he and the spirit had named the shapes they saw in the clouds overhead. The spirit spoke to him now through the music just as it had back then through the rustle of the leaves of its tree and the chattering of the birds who made nests in the tree's branches.

The young man had closed his eyes, his fingers moving on the strings so gently that Beau heard the music as much with his mind as his ears. The spirit's magic enhanced the music, and together they told a story that Beau had only guessed at.

The spirit's tree had been murdered by one of the greedy,

evil men from across the sea. He had mutilated the tree's body, chopping off its branches, burning off its bark. But the fire he'd started consumed too much of the wood, growing large and uncontrollable. When the spirit's enslaver had tried to put it out, the fire had killed him instead.

The remains of the tree had smoldered for days until rains put the fire out. The remains of the great tree rested at the bottom of a pile of ash while time passed and the spirit despaired of spending eternity trapped inside the charred body of its tree.

Then one day the tree had been discovered by a kindly man who worked with wood. He cleaned away the ash and soot and discovered the heart of the tree which had not been touched by the fire. He took the heart of the tree with him, intent on using the wood to carve toys for his neighbor's children.

The toymaker had been the young man's grandfather.

He had no magic of his own and was unaware of the wounded spirit that still lived in the wood. For its part, the spirit had been so abused by men that it kept silent as the toymaker took small bits of the tree and carved them into toys.

Slowly the spirit began to see that the toymaker was not an evil man. How could an evil man bring such joy to children? The spirit watched as parts of its tree made children happy, just like the spirit tree had been happy when Beau climbed its branches.

The spirit eventually came out of hiding. It began to feel joy itself. If it couldn't live in the great forest, it could still live in the remains of its tree for the toymaker only took small bits of the tree when he created his toys.

That's when the lawgiver came into their lives.

She had been a beautiful elf who carried a talisman of her own. The talisman had helped her find the spirit, but instead of an enslaver, she found a kind and gentle man.

Her talisman insisted that the toymaker be punished for he

claimed ownership of what remained of the spirit tree. The lawgiver refused, for she had fallen in love with the toymaker. She buried the talisman deep in the earth and left her lawgiver ways behind.

She made a life with the toymaker, and together they raised the young man's father and his uncles and aunts. The toymaker gifted each with a special toy made from the spirit tree's wood, but instead of causing the spirit grief as its tree was slowly carved away, the love the lawgiver and the toymaker shared gave the spirit joy. It shared that joy with the toymaker in the only way it could—by encouraging him to make something special for the love of his life.

And so the toymaker had made his wife the guitar with the last of the wood that the spirit inhabited.

Whenever the toymaker played the guitar he had crafted, the spirit sang through the strings, just as it sang to Beau now.

Had the lawgiver known that the spirit was happy? She must have. Like all elves, she could commune with the spirit trees.

By the time the young man had finished playing, Beau's heart was so full that he thought it might break.

He had found his old friend, and instead of the insane spirit he had feared he would have to kill, he'd discovered a spirit filled with joy. It would be the height of cruel to destroy the guitar now, even if such an act set the spirit free. The guitar was the last surviving part of the tree in which the spirit lived. The spirit wasn't imprisoned. It had chosen the guitar as its home.

Beau had a duty to carry out. A duty to kill this spirit as his talisman demanded.

But wasn't friendship and loyalty a far greater duty?

The enslaver Beau had planned to kill was long dead. This young man and his father and grandfather before him had loved and cared for the guitar and the spirit they didn't even know lived inside. They were innocents, and innocents didn't deserve to die.

Beau stood up. He pushed his cup of whiskey across the table toward the young man.

"That was a beautiful song," he said.

The young man blinked his eyes open. He'd almost been in a trance while he played, which Beau knew was the spirit communing with him. Something the young man no doubt thought of as inspiration.

The spirit had found a new friend. Beau couldn't take that away.

"You heard that?" the young man asked. "Even over the storm?"

"I did," Beau said.

He tipped the brim of his hat at the young man and made his way to the front of the saloon. The wind still howled outside, and the talisman burned hot and angry in the pocket of his long coat.

A couple of the men inside the saloon looked up when he opened the door. The wind nearly ripped the door from his grip as it blew the hair away from his face and threatened to steal his hat.

If any of the men who'd glanced up when he'd opened the door saw the points of his ears, they didn't say anything but just went back to their drinks and their cards.

Outside the storm was fierce. Beau tasted the dry desert sand in his mouth as it pelted him, and he turned his back on it as he walked down the dirt track that passed for a street in this no-name mining town. He kept walking past the last building and into the night. His vision was excellent, and he didn't need light on this moonless night to see where he was headed.

When he came to the tailings that marked an abandoned mine, he stopped. He took the talisman from his pocket. The markings on it practically thrummed with unused magic and the demands that Beau do his duty.

Dark creatures lived in the deep tunnels of abandoned mines. Creatures who ate magic and ground rock between diamond-sharp teeth. They roamed the desert freely on nights like this when men were huddled inside, out of the storm. Beau could feel their eyes on him, although they wouldn't approach him. Even creatures of the night recognized a lawgiver when they saw one.

Beau removed the leather strap from the talisman and held the stone up to the storm. It had been a part of him ever since he'd become a lawgiver like his father before him. Ever since he'd left his home in search of evil men who'd done evil deeds to gentle spirits who'd never meant anyone harm.

The talisman was the embodiment of the duty Beau had sworn to perform when he'd taken his oath as a lawgiver. If he failed to carry out that duty, he would never be able to return home again.

Was that really such a high price to pay for the life of his friend?

He drew back his arm and used all his strength to throw the talisman as hard as he could into the night. As it flew away from him, caught by the fierce winds and battered by the sand, he imagined he heard it scream just as he heard the creatures of the night howling in glee.

Beau turned up the collar of his long coat and hunched his shoulders against the wind. The next town was day's walk away. From there he could go north, into the high mountains beyond. He'd heard tales of a beautiful mountain lake surrounded by tall pines. He might even be able to lose himself there. To live the rest of his days in the shadow world of magic folk that men knew nothing about.

Even men who had a touch of magic themselves.

Beau smiled as he thought of the young guitar player and the spirit who inspired him. The spirit who'd been Beau's friend.

He let the storm swallow him as he walked into the night, leaving friendship and duty behind, with only the memory of the sweet guitar music to keep him company.

It was more than enough. It would be more than enough for the rest of his days.

ABOUT THE AUTHOR

Annie Reed is a frequent contributor to Fiction River as well as Pulphouse Fiction Magazine. Her award-winning story "The Color of Guilt," chosen as one of *The Best Crime and Mystery Stories of 2016*, originally appeared in *Fiction River: Hidden in Crime*. She frequently writes stories (including her popular Diz and Dee Mysteries) set in the fictional Pacific Northwest city of Moretown Bay, a place where magic and modern life go hand in hand. Annie also writes sweet romance under the pen name Liz McKnight.

Find out more about Annie at:
www.annie-reed.com

TO SPEAK TO THE GODS

JAMIE FERGUSON

Liana sat on the stone steps of the terrace facing the wide, open temple square on the island of Meligunis, a pile of straw to her left and the small stack of straw mats she'd woven so far to her right. The Sun was high in the bright, azure sky, but the grapevines and bougainvillea covering the trellis she sat under shielded her from the bright rays. A soft, warm breeze carried the salty tang of the sea in to mix with the sweetness of the mint growing in whitewashed pots. Bits of straw had mysteriously found their way inside her linen tunic, and were making her chore even less pleasant than normal.

She would rather do something like herd goats or sheep, like her cousin Tiam, but on Liana's last birthday her mother had made it clear it wasn't proper for a fifteen-year-old girl to spend her days out with the livestock, even if she'd finished her work for the day. Doing so just wasn't proper, her mother said. Liana would soon be old enough to be married, and who would want to marry a girl who smelled like sheep? Besides, they needed the mats to dry the olives that would soon be ripe. And once the mats were done, there would be weaving.

The list of 'proper' chores was endless.

So instead of spending her afternoons on the upper slopes of the little volcanic island, as she had for the past several years, Liana had to focus on more domestic tasks, like weaving what she was sure was more drying mats than any of the villages in the island chain could possibly need in her lifetime. Her little brother Ruan now helped Tiam with the animals instead.

Liana brushed a piece of straw off her neck and looked across the square. She didn't want to get married, and certainly not to Nandru, the man she'd overheard her parents talking about last night as a possible husband once she was a little older. Nandru was a few years older than Liana, and was nice enough, even if he couldn't seem to talk about anything but carving and polishing obsidian. He would be a good husband

and father—but the last thing Liana wanted to do was marry and have children.

What Liana really wanted was to be a priestess. No one told the priestesses what to do. No one made them stay home and do silly girl chores. They did important things, like talk to the gods.

A low rumble came from the mountain that jutted out of the sea to the northeast.

Liana grinned. Struognuli, the god of fire, agreed with her.

Or at least she liked to think he did.

She glanced over at the temple. It was made from stone, lava, and pumice, like all of the buildings in the village, but its roof was high and domed. It was painted a white so bright it glowed in the sunlight. The square, blocky houses that surrounded it were white or peach or pink. The altar that stood in front of the temple was made from rock as black as charcoal, and flower petals were scattered on the stones surrounding it to honor the Goddess.

Several old men sat under an oleander tree near the open temple doors. They were having an animated discussion about a broken ceramic bowl one of them had found in the remains of the village that lay higher up on the slopes of the mountain, a village so ancient no one living remembered anything about it. Occasionally the men would all stop and stare at the bowl in silence for a moment before resuming their conversation.

Liana tied a knot in the last piece of straw and set down her seventh finished mat. It was going to be a long day. She wrinkled her nose at the stack of mats and picked up another handful of straw, then almost dropped it as Tiam sprinted past her, running down the pavestones as if he'd been hit by a cinder spewed from Struognuli's mouth. He skidded to a stop in front of the group of men, but was so out of breath he could only sputter incoherently. Finally he gave up and bent over, inhaling great gasps of air.

This was unusual. A chill of excitement ran down her spine. Tiam had been high up on the mountain with his sheep, maybe high enough to see the volcano on the next island do something interesting, like when it had spouted fire last fall the day after her birthday. Their own volcano was pretty settled—it's god let out big puffs of smoke now and again, but that was it. No one left alive was old enough to remember when the god had been angry last.

She dropped the straw and trotted across the square just in time to hear her cousin speak his first word.

"Boats!" He waved his hand in the direction of the ocean, which was certainly where one might expect to find boats.

"Of course there are," one of the old men said. He handed Tiam a ceramic flask.

Tiam took a gulp, then spit the liquid out on the stones. He coughed and put his hand to his mouth, his eyes wide. The men chuckled.

"Where do you think we get fish?" another man asked.

A few other villagers joined the group, including the chief. Tiam blinked, then straightened his shoulders and returned the flask.

"These aren't fishing boats," Tiam said. "They're big, higher in the water than a fishing boat, or any of the craft the traders use. There are five boats. Each has many people on them, and they are all flying red and blue flags."

Liana glanced out toward the ocean, but she couldn't see the ships from where she stood. That flag didn't sound like the flags flying from any of the ships that normally passed through the islands. Perhaps Tiam had seen people from a new land. She glanced back at her house to make sure her mother hadn't noticed she'd taken a break from weaving. So far so good.

"They're here to trade," the chief said, his deep voice strong and confident. Meligunis was not only on a busy trade path, it was also the source of black obsidian, which was much prized.

"Maybe we can sell them a ship full of capers," said one of the old men. The crowd laughed.

Liana chuckled as well. Capers, salted or pickled or fresh, grew so well on the island that everyone ate them at least once a day.

"Perhaps they do," the priestess said.

Everyone turned toward her voice. She stood in the doorway of the temple, her wrinkled face just inside the shadows, so her eyes could barely be seen. Her hair curled down to her waist, the golden-brown strands streaked with white. Her sandaled feet peeked out from underneath her flowing white robes, revealing an ankle bracelet made of small, multi-colored stones. Even at her age her she carried an energy that made her very presence commanding. It was as if the gods stood beside to her, invisible to all eyes but hers.

The chief looked away from the crowd, out toward the sea. His brow furrowed for a moment, but his face changed back to his normally confident expression so quickly that Liana decided she must have imagined it.

∽

LIANA SNEAKED AWAY from her chores long enough to watch one of the ships dock. The other four remained well out to sea, their red and blue flags flying. Four men left the boat and came to shore, where the chief and several other men from the village met them. They talked for a few minute, then began the walk up the steep hillside to the village.

Liana hurried back to her family's terrace, and watched as the chief led four of the strange men into the temple square. She was used to the traders that came to the island, but the newcomers were clearly different, and therefore interesting. Of course, anything was more interesting than weaving straw.

The strangers' hair was black, and they all had dark brown eyes and thick, curly beards. Three of them wore short linen tunics; their leader's was longer, and was made of patterned fabric. He wore a cap with a topknot, and over his left shoulder was thrown a mantle of rich purple, a fascinating color Liana never seen before.

They asked the chief about everything the island had to offer: obsidian, olives, artichokes, pumice stone, salt, mulberries, wine. They even asked about capers, which immensely amused the group of old men who had stayed in their spot under the oleander to eavesdrop long after they would normally have headed back to their homes for the midday meal.

Liana finished weaving her tenth mat of the day and reached out for another handful of straw, her eyes fixed on the strangers. She stifled a squeal as her hand touched something warm and soft.

"Surprise," Tiam said. He sat down next to her on the warm stone.

"You scared me half to death," Liana said, keeping her voice low so that it didn't carry out into the square. She smacked him in the shoulder. "What are you doing here? Where's your flock?"

"Your brother's watching them," he said. He grinned. "I told him he'd learned enough about herding to spend the afternoon handling the sheep on his own. He's very proud of himself."

"That's mean," Liana said. She poked him with a piece of straw. "Since you've handed off your own work, why don't you help me with these stupid mats?"

"No way," he said. "That's women's work. I'm a *man*."

"You're a *boy*," she said. She squinted at where the strangers sat in the shade. The one who wore the cap was inspecting a chunk of obsidian.

"I'm sixteen," Tiam said. "And no matter what my age, I know those men aren't traders."

Liana looked at her cousin, her eyes narrowed. "Why? Just because their boats are larger than any we've seen before?"

"It's not just the size," he said. "It's the way they're designed. Did you notice the bows?"

Liana shook her head. She'd sneaked out to peek at the boats earlier, before the one had docked, but she hadn't paid attention to the construction the way her cousin had.

"Well," Tiam said. "They're clearly designed to move fast. And each boat carries at least twenty men. That's far too many for them to be able to fit much cargo on board."

Liana stared at the strangers. They'd moved into the shade of an olive tree, and were sitting on the ground. The priestess came out of the temple carrying an amphora filled with honey mead. She nodded to the chief and began filling cups for the strangers, her long, honey and white curls almost touching the ground as she bent down to hand each man a cup.

The newcomers stared at the priestess as if they'd never seen a woman before. Even from across the square, the expressions on the men's faces made Liana feel uncomfortable. The leader made a comment about how they'd never before seen anyone with such light-colored hair.

That seemed odd. Many people in the islands had hair of light brown, or even blonde. Where did these come from?

"So if you don't think they're traders," Liana said. "Then why do you suppose they came here? Maybe they're explorers." Yes, that sounded right. That would explain why they were intrigued by so many everyday things.

Tiam shook his head. "I don't know," he said.

∼

THE CHIEF INVITED the newcomers to stay on the island and enjoy the village's hospitality while they worked out the details of what the two parties might trade. They agreed, and some of the men and women of the town attended a small feast with the strangers at the chief's house that evening.

Liana tried to slip away to eavesdrop on the strangers after the evening meal with her family, but several of her mother's friends stopped by to visit, and Liana was stuck spending her evening with a group of chattering women. They were fascinated by the purple mantle the leader of the newcomers wore, and there was a great deal of speculation about what the strangers might be wearing underneath their tunics—if they wore anything at all.

Liana tried not to roll her eyes at the conversation. Who cared what kind of undergarments the strangers wore? Was she going to turn into someone like this once she was older and married? All the more reason to be a priestess.

Except, of course, that the village already had one.

THE NEXT MORNING Liana was shaken awake. She opened her eyes to see Tiam. He pressed a finger to his mouth, then motioned for her to follow him. She stepped out on the terrace and rubbed her eyes. The sun was just peeking up to the east, and the sky was dark blue and gray, with faint streaks of pink.

"What's going on?" Liana asked. "Why did you wake me up?" She shivered in the morning chill.

"The boats that were moored just offshore at sunset are gone," he said.

"So?" Liana rubbed the goose bumps on her arms. She glanced at the large pile of straw that lay on the stones. It was going to be another long, tedious day, and now she'd had to start it way too soon. "They're probably visiting the other villages to talk with them about trading as well."

"Maybe," Tiam said. "But I feel as if something is wrong. And I don't think anyone else is concerned."

Liana took a deep breath. Tiam might be annoying at times, like any boy, but he wasn't stupid. He often knew when one of his flock was about to give birth, and had an uncanny knack for knowing which ewes would need his help and which would do fine on their own.

"If something is wrong, then we need to find out what," she said. "But how?"

"I will watch them when I can," he said.

"As will I," Liana said.

For the next week Liana and Tiam took advantage of every opportunity to follow the newcomers and spy on them from a distance. The men hiked around the volcano, muttering to each other and holding their noses against the smell of sulfur whenever they ran across a fumarole. They walked through the olive grove, and appeared to be counting the trees. They wandered about the village, asking the old women odd questions, like how long capers should be left in the sunlight to dry, or what herbs they put in their soup.

They seemed peaceable, but they always carried their knives, and they always stayed near by each other.

One night several of the men of the island met the chief's home to talk about trading with the newcomers. Liana and Tiam sneaked out after their mothers had gone to bed. They sat in the dark under an oleander tree, as still as could be, and tried to make out what the village men were saying. They learned that the leader of the newcomers was named Drian, and that he had offered to trade some of the violet fabric for obsidian—but at an exorbitant price.

The Moon was almost full. It lit up the courtyard with its

silvery light until a cloud passed in front of it, temporarily hiding the brightness. Liana stiffened as she heard a small noise. She and her cousin froze as still as if they were statues. They watched one of the strangers walk up in the darkness, as quiet as a cat chasing a mouse. He peered in the stone window of the stable, careful to keep his head back lest the village men spot him.

After a few minutes he turned and looked directly at where the two cousins sat in the shadows. A beam of moonlight shone on the man's face, brightening his features—but his eyes stayed dark, and looked like the sockets of a skull. Chills ran down Liana's spine. The man grinned, then strutted away without a sound.

The next day they told the high priestess what they'd seen. She nodded, but her wrinkled face was unconcerned.

"They have come from a far-away land," she said in her rich, throaty voice. Liana hoped someday her own voice would sound even half as lovely. "They are establishing relations for trades. I know. I have spoken with the gods."

Liana wanted to feel reassured by the priestess' words.

But Tiam remained concerned, and that troubled her.

∼

Two mornings later, the other boats returned.

This time they moored right off the shore. The four men who'd been staying in the village met with the chief, then headed down to the water and got back on their boat. The men who'd stayed on the boat rowed it out to sea where it met the other boats.

That evening the chief called the villagers to the temple square. Liana and Tiam leaned their backs against her family's terrace wall and waited for the town folk to assemble.

The temple was made from stone, lava, and pumice, like all of the buildings in the village, but its roof was high and domed. It was painted a white so bright it glowed in the sunlight. The square, blocky houses that surrounded it were white or peach or pink. The altar that stood in front of the temple was made from rock as black as charcoal, and flower petals were scattered on the stones surrounding it to honor the Goddess.

The priestess joined the chief next to the altar stone. She nodded at him, then they both turned to face the villagers.

"My people," the chief said. "We face a grave problem."

A murmur spread through the crowd. The chief's face was stolid. The high priestess' was implacable, as if she were about to begin performing a ceremony or rite.

"It's the boat men," Tiam whispered to Liana. His breath was hot and wet. She grimaced and wiped her ear.

"It can't be," Liana said. She glared at him. "The priestess talked with the gods. Those men are just here to trade."

She wanted her words to be true, but her stomach fluttered as though it were filled with butterflies. The gods could certainly be complicated. They often answered merely the question that was asked, and did not always offer other information, even when that information would have been much more useful. And sometimes their answers were so cryptic as to be worse than no answers at all. The priestess had explained that this was a failing of mankind, that the gods spoke truth but that humans were not always able to understand.

Liana wondered if she would be able to understand the gods any better if she were to become a priestess herself.

The chief cleared his throat. "The men who came from elsewhere ... they want to take our village."

There was much murmuring. "How can they take our village?" someone said. "We *live* here."

"They have offered us the option to stay," the chief said. "But as slaves. Or we can leave. Or ..."

The rising Moon, a sliver larger since last night, was bright in the sky behind the temple.

"Or they will kill us," he said.

Liam squeezed Tiam's arm. They huddled together while the villagers shouted. The chief and the priestess stood next to one another in silence, waiting for the hubbub to subside.

A woman stood up. Her long brown hair was streaked with white. "What about the other villages?" she asked.

"They face the same choice," the chief said. He took a deep breath. "The strangers have told me this, and I consulted with my fellow chiefs on Meligunis. One of them has heard similar stories from the village on our sister island to the east."

More shouting occurred.

The high priestess moved to stand in front of the altar. During ceremonies she stood behind it, or on it, but never in front of it. The crowd grew quiet. A tiny gust of wind brushed her long, gold and white hair. A lock of it wrapped around her forearm, like one of the snakes she used in the ceremony of Sarna. She raised her hands, palms upward. The villagers quieted.

"I say we fight," the chief said. "We cannot give up our village. We will not be slaves again. Never again. Our forefathers fought for their freedom, many generations ago. We must not go back to being slaves. And -" He paused and looked at the crowd, meeting the gaze of person after person. "We can't leave. There is nowhere to go. Drian and his men intend to take over all of the islands, not just our own."

Liana pressed up even closer against Tiam. He smelled like sheep, which was normally comforting... but not tonight.

~

The strangers had given the village three days. Three days to either vacate or prepare for war.

Or to agree to become slaves.

Liana's mother decided it was time to clean the house from top to bottom, so Liana was kept busy—but the vast number of chores she was assigned did nothing to quell her fears. She didn't want to be a slave, and she didn't know how to fight. Neither did most of the men and women in the village, for that matter.

Sure, they sold obsidian, and craftsmen like Nandru carved it into knives before sale for customers who didn't want to carve their own. But theirs was a trading village, their people peaceable. The village—and all the other villages on the islands—would crumble under any attack.

Tiam had the sharpest eyes of anyone, and he'd counted at least two hundred men total on the boats. He said he could see their knives and some other type of weapon; a long knife, maybe three times the size of a regular dagger.

Liana couldn't see any of these no matter how much she squinted, but her eyes weren't nearly as good at seeing things far away as Tiam's, at least not for the past year or so.

The cousins spent the day after the chief's announcement on the hillside just up past the town, alternating between staring out at the ships and watching the strangers set up a camp by the shore. After some time Tiam went up the hill to check on Ruan and the sheep. Liana wrapped her arms around her knees and glared at the boats. How dare these men threaten her people? There had to be something they could do. Maybe there was even something *she* could do.

Struognuli rumbled, as if he were saying say yes. Yes, Liana, there is something you can do.

He was a god, the most important god of the islands. If he believed she could make a difference, then perhaps she could.

Liana took a deep breath, then stood up and brushed bits of grass off her dress. She looked up the hillside. She could barely make out Tiam and Ruan's dark shapes in the midst of the grayish-white dots of sheep. She didn't know what she was going to do, but she knew she needed Tiam's help.

∼

THAT EVENING TIAM sneaked down by the strangers' camp on the beach to see if he could learn anything that might help them understand what Struognuli had been hinting at. Liana had wanted to go, but Tiam had argued that he was the more nimble of the two. After an argument about that, he'd pointed out that his eyesight was better, especially at night, and Liana begrudgingly gave in.

After her parents had fallen asleep she tiptoed out to the terrace and waited for Tiam's return. It was dusk, the clear sky the soft blue-black color it turned after the Sun had run off to his home so that the Moon couldn't catch him. Liana wondered what would happen if the Moon ever caught the Sun.

What if Tiam was caught by the strange men? Would they kill him? Make him their slave? Liana bit her lip and stared up into the sky, then jumped at a small sound.

"It's just me," Tiam whispered as he walked around the corner. He padded up the steps to the terrace, his feet bare feet. His feet were bare. He set his sandals on the stone and sat down next to her.

"Did you find anything?"

He nodded. His features were gray and silver in the moonlight.

"Yes," he said. "They came to conquer us because their goddess Athart spoke to their leader, Drian, in a vision. She told him to sail east, far away from their native lands, and that he would find islands that belonged to her, islands filled with riches unknown to his people."

"Did she tell him to kill the people on these islands?"

"I don't think so," Tiam said. "I expected to hear the men say that, but they spoke only of the riches Drian had predicted they'd find, and how he was favored by Athart because she does not often speak to mortal men."

"Athart..." Liana said. She furrowed her brow. "That name sounds similar to our goddess, Athata. Do you suppose their goddess is the same as ours?"

Tiam thought for a moment. "I suppose it might," he said. "We know our people came from the east many moons ago. It could be that our forefathers and those of these men were the same, far back in time."

Liana looked out at where Struognuli sat in the sea. Even with the brightness of the moonlight, the sky was still dark enough to see the red glow at the top of the volcano. She clasped her hands together so tightly they hurt.

"What do you think?" she whispered to the god.

"What?" Tiam said.

Liana ignored him and watched the volcano.

Struognuli spit out a burst of crimson, the molten rock making lines that arced high in the sky, then fell into the ocean below. Liana could almost hear the hiss the fire made as it hit the cool water.

So Struognuli agreed. Liana smiled.

"I have a plan," she said.

∽

Two days later Drian came to the temple square to meet the chief. Drian had brought more men with him this time—Liana counted at least ten, although it was difficult to be sure from her perch in the oleander tree, because the leaves obscured her view. She wore a tunic made of the softest cotton, dyed red as the fire Struognuli spewed into the air, and her face was painted with the markings of the goddess Athata.

The chief stood in front of the altar. His eyes were puffy from worry and lack of sleep. The priestess stood next to him, her wrinkled face calm and confident in contrast.

"Greetings, my lord," Drian said.

"And to you as well," the chief said.

"Have you made your decision?" Drian asked.

The chief took a deep breath. "I beg of you," he said. "We are traders, not fighters. We have nowhere to go. We do not wish to become slaves, and we don't stand a chance against your men."

Drian waved a hand. "That is not my concern," he said. "I asked you for a decision. Which is your choice?"

The chief opened his mouth, then closed it. He looked at the priestess. She kept her eyes on Drian, and said nothing.

"Then I will decide for you," Drian said. "I take —"

"Drian!" Liana yelled. She leapt down from the tree and strode across the square. Every eye was on her—confused, surprised, but not yet understanding. "It is I, Athart," she said, careful to use the voice she'd practiced with Tiam for the past two days—her tone one of command, of power, just like a goddess would sound.

She heard her mother's voice from somewhere behind her, but ignored it just like she ignored the gasps and exclamations that came from around the square. The priestess turned to watch Liana approach, an expression of shock and admiration on her face—just as they'd agreed when Liana had come to her with the plan the day before.

"Little girl," Drian said, a smirk on his face. "Are you in that much hurry to become a slave?"

She reached the altar and leapt up on top of it. The dark

volcanic rock was warm beneath her bare feet. The priestess knelt on the ground in front of the altar. The chief looked at her, then at Liana, unsure what to do.

"I am the goddess Athart," Liana said. "I am using this child to speak to you. Do you not recognize me?" She smiled. "I have favored you in the past, and by appearing in this way I am granting you a gift that I do not often give to mortal men. It has been over a century since I cared enough about a human to manifest in their presence."

Drian blinked. Excellent. He wasn't convinced yet, but he was starting to wonder.

"I asked you to find my islands," Liana said. "Did I not?"

Drian glanced at his men, then looked back up at Liana. He nodded.

"And what else did I say?"

He took a deep breath. "You said... To find your lands, and that they'd be filled with riches that my people had never heard of before."

Liana glared down at him. "Did I tell you to hurt the people you found there?"

"You told me there would be riches," Drian said.

"That is not an answer," Liana said. "These islands are my islands, and these people are my people. They worship me here as Athata, as I instructed them to do many years ago—just like I ordered your people to call me Athart."

Drian shook his head. "I am confused, my lady," he said.

"I can see that you are," Liana said. She smiled. "But everything is clear. You have found what I sent you to seek. You are special to me. I wanted you to find these islands—*and* these people—so that you could establish trade, and thereby gain wealth and power."

"Trade?" he said.

"Trade," Liana said, her voice firm. "I will visit you again, my dear Drian. But only if you do as I command. It is not often that a mortal has a goddess by his side."

Drian nodded. "I am sorry, my lady. I misunderstood. Please forgive me."

Liana smiled, trying to convey all the warmth and benevolence a goddess would bestow on a favored subject.

"I forgive you," she said. "Until we meet again."

Liana raised her arms in the air, then pretended to collapse in a way that made it look as if she'd fallen off the altar on to the stone below. She lay there in a crumpled heap. The priestess came over and helped her up.

"What happened?" Liana said, her voice soft and weak.

"You were the mouthpiece for the goddess Athata," the priestess said.

"I don't understand," Liana said. She shot a glance at Drian, who was stroking his chin. "Why am I wearing these robes? Why am I on the ground?"

Drian raised his chin, then turned to the chief.

"I am sorry for the misunderstanding," Drian said. "I would like to discuss the establishment of trade between our peoples." He glanced at Liana. "For real, this time."

A soft, low sound came from the northeast. Liana smiled.

Struognuli was happy.

ABOUT THE AUTHOR

Jamie focuses on getting into the minds and hearts of her characters, whether she's writing about a saloon girl in the American West, a man who discovers the barista he's in love with is a naiad, or a ghost who haunts the house she was killed in—even though that house no longer exists. Jamie lives in Colorado, and spends her free time in a futile quest to wear out her two border collies since she hasn't given in and gotten them their own herd of sheep.

Find her online:
JamieFerguson.com

- facebook.com/jamie.ferguson.author
- twitter.com/jamie_ferguson
- instagram.com/jamie.ferguson.author
- pinterest.com/jamieauthor
- bookbub.com/authors/jamie-ferguson

UNCOLLECTED ANTHOLOGY

Short fiction that
redefines the boundaries
of urban & contemporary fantasy.

Unexpected Histories: Issue 28

Visit www.uncollectedanthology.com to see the list of all stories in this issue of Uncollected Anthology. Read them individually or buy the bundle at your favorite online distributor.

Missed past issues? They too are available by issue or in full year bundles. UA started in 2014, so an abundance of incredible reading awaits! All anthology bundles are available in ebook and print.

To keep up with the new releases, learn more about your current UA authors and past guest authors, visit the UA website at www.uncollectedanthology.com and signup for our newsletter.

> "The idea behind this anthology series is a little different...what can't be denied is that something is working with this new method."
>
> **- Charles de Lint**

UNCOLLECTED ANTHOLOGY MEMBER WEBSITES

http://www.dayledermatis.com/blog/uncollected-anthology-series/
    http://www.leahcutter.com/uncollected-anthology/
    http://anniereed.wordpress.com/uncollected-anthology/
    http://michelelang.com/
    http://rebeccasenese.com/series/uncollected-anthology/
    http://jamieferguson.com
    http://www.robertjeschonek.com
    https://www.stefonmears.com
    http://wonderlandpress.com/
    www.debbiemumford.com
    www.jasonadams.info
    www.karikilgore.com

Made in the USA
Columbia, SC
04 August 2022